"Are you a philanderer, Max?" Amy asked

She saw that secret smile grow along his firm lips, lips that now were so very close.

"Of course! If you hadn't shot off when you were seventeen, you would have realized it by now." He came even closer.

"Max!" There was real panic in her voice, but it didn't stop him. His lips brushed hers gently. "You owe me the feeling of safety. Don't forget that I was a little girl here."

"Little girls grow up, thank heaven," he said in a murmur. "You're secure, Blue Eyes! Kissing me isn't going to change your life dramatically, especially with all your experience with men."

It would, though, and Amy knew it. Yet it was impossible to get away, even if she had been really trying....

PATRICIA WILSON used to live in Yorkshire, England, but with her children all grown up, she decided to give up her teaching position there and accompany her husband on an extended trip to Spain. Their travels are providing her with plenty of inspiration for her romance writing.

Books by Patricia Wilson

HARLEQUIN PRESENTS
934 —THE FINAL PRICE
1062 —A LINGERING MELODY
1086 —THE ORTIGA MARRIAGE
1110 —A MOMENT OF ANGER
1125 —IMPOSSIBLE BARGAIN
1150 —BELOVED INTRUDER

HARLEQUIN ROMANCE
2856 —BRIDE OF DIAZ

Don't miss any of our special offers. Write to us at the following address for information on our newest releases.

Harlequin Reader Service
901 Fuhrmann Blvd., P.O. Box 1397, Buffalo, NY 14240
Canadian address: P.O. Box 603,
Fort Erie, Ont. L2A 5X3

PATRICIA WILSON

a certain affection

Harlequin Books

TORONTO • NEW YORK • LONDON
AMSTERDAM • PARIS • SYDNEY • HAMBURG
STOCKHOLM • ATHENS • TOKYO • MILAN

Harlequin Presents first edition May 1989
ISBN 0-373-11174-6

Original hardcover edition published in 1988
by Mills & Boon Limited

CHAPTER ONE

'WELL, would you believe it? Max is getting married!'

Amy Tremaine looked across at her aunt Joan for a second and then resumed her hearty breakfast.

'No, I wouldn't believe it, not unless I actually saw the event take place. Even then, I'd be suspicious.'

Maxwell St Clair had enjoyed his freedom for far too long to give it up now, and Amy tried to imagine the sort of person who would be able to lure him into tying the knot. She gave the idea up altogether almost at once.

'Dorothy says he brings her home all the time. She says she's sure it's in the air, though nothing has actually been said.' Aunt Joan glanced back at the letter to check that there were no further clues, and Amy smiled triumphantly.

'Aha! What did I tell you? It's Aunt Dorothy off again, matchmaking! Anyone who captures Max will have to drop a net over him and stun him with a heavy object!'

'Dorothy says this girl is very sweet. He'll have to marry one day,' Aunt Joan predicted, 'everybody does!'

'You didn't,' Amy reminded her, hastily finishing her breakfast and glancing at the clock.

'Well, I'm too smart for that,' Aunt Joan said slyly, with a quick knowing glance at her.

'Me, too, so don't go giving me any of your looks. Got to dash, darling. I've got 3B first thing—the horror of it!'

'We're invited up next week,' Aunt Joan said quickly as

Amy got to the door. 'Northumberland in this glorious weather—it's going to be heavenly!'

'Oh, you know I can't go.' Amy felt guilty. She hated to disappoint her aunt, and she was putting off a visit yet again. 'I know the school closes for the summer, but I've got a match arranged for mid-week, and then there's Clive. We're going to a concert at the Albert Hall and then . . .'

'Amy, Dorothy expects us to go! You used to love it up there and it would do you so much good to get away. I'm going for a good holiday, but you don't need to stay more than a week. Surely that school team can cope without you just this once? As to Clive . . .'

'Now, now, least said soonest mended!' warned Amy. She had a fair idea of her aunt's opinion of Clive. 'Listen, I've got to go. I'll think about it and maybe manage the weekend, or perhaps from Monday to Wednesday. How about that?'

'You said exactly the same thing last time, and then you never came!' her aunt accused. 'I can't understand why you've stopped wanting to go. You spent such a lot of time there before you went to college, and then since that first year you've never set foot in the place. It really must be hurtful to Dorothy, and to the others. You got on so very well with Sebastian and Bernice, and as to Max, there was always a certain affection between you, even when you were a child. What am I to tell Dorothy?'

'Tell her I'll go Monday to Wednesday.' Amy glanced at her aunt's face. 'All right—a week, you bully!'

'You've made a promise, Amy!' Aunt Joan warned her sternly, and she grinned back cheerfully, crossing her heart and holding up her hand before closing the door with a bang and racing down the street towards the station.

Her ability to run came in useful yet again, and she just managed to leap on the train before it left and sink thankfully into a seat. Her short, thick black hair was a little wild now, not the crisp, shining halo that had been around her head when she left the house, and her bright blue eyes were even more blue in her flushed and lovely face, but she was in fine physical condition and she hardly noticed the run.

Her mind, though, wandered back to the conversation with Aunt Joan as the steady rattle of the train and the pale, strained faces of the other passengers soon lost interest for her.

She had lived in London with her aunt Joan since her parents had died in a sailing accident when she was almost eleven years old. Of course, Aunt Dorothy had lived there too then, the two sisters devoted to each other as they had also been devoted to her mother. It was through Dorothy that the rather grand life at the house in Northumberland had penetrated their lives.

Dorothy was secretary to Benedict St Clair, a Member of Parliament for that part of the country for years, and naturally he spent a good deal of time in his constituency, taking Dorothy with him regularly. He was a widower. Dorothy had never married, so that when she suddenly announced her forthcoming marriage to Benedict St Clair, Amy had been childishly shocked, although Aunt Joan had confided in her that she had expected it all along.

To the eleven-year-old Amy, though, Aunt Dorothy, at forty, had been an old woman, and she had been not a little embarrassed and alarmed to discover that she had

been chosen to be a bridesmaid. It was her introduction to
Northumberland, to Belmore House, to the St Clair
family—and to Maxwell. She gazed out of the window
and found a smile creeping across her face, a smile of
reminiscence. What had Aunt Joan said? A certain
affection? Yes, there had been that.

Her hair had been long then, almost to her waist, and
she had worn a blue dress that picked up the colour of her
eyes. She had been so very nervous, small and slight for
her almost twelve years and grateful for the help of
Bernice St Clair, who, at seventeen, had been the chief
bridesmaid.

Always theatrical, her aunt Dorothy had arranged for
the petite, almost tiny Amy to walk from the church in
front of the newly wed pair, a basket of flowers on her arm
and strict instructions drilled into her to toss the rose petals
and tiny rosebuds delicately from side to side as she walked
down the aisle.

Encumbered by the long, full skirt of her dress,
embarrassed by the circlet of flowers on her black, shining
hair, Amy had been more at pains to remain upright than
to take careful aim, and it was inevitable that after
negotiating the altar steps she should toss one very large
handful of petals and buds into the lap of one of the chief
guests, an old and dignified maiden aunt of the groom.

Staring, appalled, into the indignant old eyes, Amy had
hastily re-assessed Aunt Dorothy's age. There was old, and
then again there was old! Her anxious gaze had lifted as
she regained her stride and found herself staring straight
into two laughing grey eyes, a tanned, handsome face, a
man with dark brown hair and firmly carved lips that
were now twitching with amusement. She realised that she

had seen him before, in the flurry of preparations before everyone had left for church, and she frowned at him with a small and angry dignity as he winked at her and turned to his companion to share his laughter.

It did not help matters, and she could not fail to notice that he too was old, he could even be twenty-two or three—she was not very good at guessing that sort of thing. Everybody was old, she noticed as she made her way to the church door with her soft lips tightly controlled and mutiny growing inside her.

It was a relief when Bernice took the flowers from her and whispered, 'Well done!' Amy liked Bernice, and her aunt Dorothy hugged her and took her hand, showing her where to stand for the wedding photographs. The man was there too, still looking at her with amused eyes, and when he was not in the photograph, he came closer and took shots of her with his own camera, even walking round to get her from different angles. He really scared her then.

There was a big marquee on the lawn at Belmore House, a very splendid buffet luncheon, and Amy was free. Her aunt Joan saw to it that she was fed, and then they all talked, and talked and talked! The long dress was still a great nuisance and she had a desire to tuck it up and forget about it, but one glance at the grown-ups, who seemed to number hundreds, decided her against that rather daring scheme. The orange juice was good, though, and it was hot inside the marquee. She took a glass very carefully from a waiter and then turned away, horrified, when she bumped into a tall man who stood with his back to her.

The juice spilled all down the back of his jacket and on to his dark trouser legs, and Amy simply stared at the havoc she had caused, hardly daring to breathe when he looked round in amazement.

'So it's the Cornish pixie! I might have known!' He looked down at her from a great towering height, as the waiter hastily mopped him up and the clear grey eyes seemed to mesmerise her.

'I—I'm sorry!' She couldn't think that any ordinary apology would get her out of this particular fix, and he looked very stern.

'So you should be! How about if I spank you, now that you're a member of my family?'

'I'm not! I'm not at all!' Amy got out hastily, wondering when he was going to reach for her and lift her up by the hair.

'Your aunt just married my father, doesn't that make you a relative of mine?' he asked from his great height, and she shook her head.

'I'm not sure, but I hope not.' Now that he was not about to beat her immediately, her nerve was somewhat restored, and she met his gaze fearlessly. 'I don't think I'd like it. You called me a Cornish pixie!'

'Well, you're so small, and you have that accent.' He crouched down beside her as she stared at him stubbornly. 'Your aunt Dorothy told me that you were born and bred in Cornwall.' His eyes moved over her hair. 'Black Cornish—isn't that what they call people like you? Doesn't everyone else have red hair?'

'We vary!' she said pertly, her small chin coming up. 'My father was dark too but I had friends of all sorts of hair colouring.' Pain flashed across her eyes at the thought of her father. It was still very close to her, and the man's grey eyes softened incredibly.

'Do you miss the sea, Amy?' She was surprised he knew her name, and she nodded, looking away, but he tilted her firm little chin. 'We have a pretty good coastline here. Now that your aunt Dorothy lives here, you'll be coming up often and you can go to the sea every day if you like, if you can forgive us for being old.'

He laughed at her red-faced surprise that he should have been able to pry into her mind, then someone called to him and he straightened up and moved away, his hand stroking her hair as he left, and he didn't seem so awful any more, even if he was old.

He was right, too. Amy did spend a lot of time at Belmore House, finding freedom in the great gardens, joy on the wild and lonely beaches and following Maxwell St Clair like a small and happy puppy whenever she saw him. She discovered too that he was very special, a sculptor, already famous, and Aunt Joan told her that his long-fingered hands were so strong because it was hard work as well as artistically demanding.

It was not too long before he assumed the proportions of a god in her mind, a god who sometimes treated her with warm-eyed affection and who sometimes ignored her. There were days when he never came out of his studio, a great converted barn that stood a little way from the house. In fact, there were times when she stayed at the house and never saw him at all, from arrival to departure, except at meal times. But always her announcements at school were that she was 'going up to see Max', never simply going to Northumberland.

Her ability to find trouble never left her, though, and the day she had found the door open at the great studio-barn lingered in her mind for a very long time. She had wandered in. She had never been told not to, and always before the great door had been shut and locked. Now, though, it was invitingly open, and Amy wandered into the high-ceilinged room that took up the whole of the place. It was like stepping into another world. There were sculptures there that towered above her, great stone or bronze pieces, some she could not understand even though they were pleasing to see. Some, though, were beautiful figures, some nude, and her face flushed that she had stepped into this secret world.

She was just about to make a hasty departure when her eye fell on a small and delicate figurine that stood on a low bench. It was grey and unpolished but beautiful, and she drew close to look at it, gasping with surprise when she saw clearly. It was her! She was in the dress that she had worn for Aunt Dorothy's wedding, and every detail was there, from the circlet of flowers on her hair to the wide tilt of her eyes.

Entranced, she reached out to touch it, too eagerly, and her hasty fingers knocked it. She tried to catch it, her heart beating frantically, but she was too late. It fell to the hard, stone floor and shattered into pieces, and Amy, after one horrified glance at the destruction, sank to the floor too, her face in her trembling hands, her hair a black curtain around her as she wept heartbrokenly.

'Amy! What on earth . . .?' Max was there almost at once, coming in through the open door, and she dared not look at him.

'I've broken it, Max! I came in here when you didn't invite me and I touched that beautiful thing. I—I broke it!' she sobbed.

He lifted her up into his arms, her slight and tiny form

cradled against him as he rocked her soothingly.

'It doesn't matter at all, poppet,' he said softly. 'You've only done what I intended to do myself.'

'You were going to break that lovely statue? It was me!' she sobbed accusingly, looking at him as if he hated her, and his handsome face creased into a smile.

'It was only my first attempt, Amy. I normally don't need two attempts, but I wanted to get that just right. In any case, it was only the mould. It would have had to go. I never make two of the same thing.'

'I don't understand.' She was sure she was really heavy, but he still held her high against his chest and his grey eyes were smiling at her. She couldn't understand at all why he wasn't furious.

'Come here, then,' he said, putting her on her feet and taking her small hand in his. 'But nobody else has seen this, so keep quiet about it. I'm only showing it to you so you won't be going away feeling guilty.'

He led her to the very back of the room, uncovering a small figure on the farthest bench, and there it was again, more beautiful than ever, cast in bronze.

'Oh, it's me!' Amy gazed at it in wonder, and he laughed softly.

'Now you know why I was taking those photographs of you at the wedding last year,' he explained. 'I had to wait quite a while to get one of your face when you weren't glaring at me.'

She looked up in astonishment and, treacherously, her blue eyes slid to the nudes, her mind working overtime, and Max shouted with laughter, lifting her up by the waist and laughing into her flushed face.

'I swear I never have!' he assured her, his grey eyes

dancing. 'Cross my heart and hope to die!'

Suddenly it was all just funny, and for a minute she was allowed to hold the delicate figurine before Max carefully wrapped it again and led her firmly from the studio. It was a shared secret and she hugged it to herself, telling not one soul.

Yes, there had been a certain affection between them, a great affection. The train pulled into the station and she stood and made her way to the door, her mind mulling over the irritation of class 3B, but her inner thoughts miles away and years away, back on the windswept coast of Northumberland, seeing a tall and powerful man chase her along the empty beach and force her, screaming and laughing, into the cold pounding sea that drenched her long black hair.

She strode through the crowds to the exit, her mind now firmly on school. Childhood was over and the dream days finished long ago. She wondered how she was going to tell Clive she was not going to the Albert Hall, after all. He might grumble, even though she knew he hadn't yet got the tickets. He might even whine—he sometimes did. She screwed up her mouth, pulling a face, getting an enraged look from the ticket collector who took it all personally, and then she was in the street, the noisy, bustling street, and the wild hills and sea of Northumberland left her mind.

Amy didn't see Clive Bradshaw until lunch time, and he was none too pleased at her news. He taught maths at the school, and was sometimes a little disapproving of Amy's lighter-than-air attitude to life.

'You can't break promises just like that, Amy!' he protested with annoyance. 'We had it all arranged, and you could go up to Northumberland later.'

'I can't, Clive. There's the match next week and the girls are expecting me to be there.'

'Well, I was expecting you to be there!' he said accusingly. 'I was going for the tickets tonight.'

'You can go with someone else,' she suggested hopefully, but that annoyed him too.

'You know I only enjoy things when you're there. I have no desire to take anyone else—unless Kitty wants to go,' he added suddenly with a spark of hope. Kitty Lambert was the other Physical Education teacher at the school, theoretically one step below Amy in the hierarchy, although Amy never took her position as Head of Department too seriously. She did most of the work, but never had to throw her slight weight about. Kitty was good and enthusiastic.

'Oh, Clive, what a good idea!' Amy gushed. 'Kitty loves that heavy music.' That got her a suspicious look, but she managed to keep a glowing face intact. The idea of sitting through an evening of dreary music had been making her feel gloomy all the week, and this was really killing two birds with one stone.

'Well, all right then, I'll ask her this afternoon,' he agreed doubtfully. 'But do realise that when you've made a commitment you have to stick to your word, Amy.'

She was getting just a little tired of Clive's forbidding little lectures, Amy thought as she made her way to the gym for the next lesson. He really was beginning to come the heavy now that they had been going out regularly with each other. It was time to bid him a fond farewell, but he could be most awkward when he wanted and it would be a little bit embarrassing as they were both in the same school. The whole thing had grown from the odd trip to the cinema, and now she found herself more or less branded as Clive's girlfriend. Maybe Kitty would step into her place? Kitty liked him. Amy liked him too, but there was no freedom with Clive and there was beginning to be a great deal of oppression.

Aunt Joan decided to go on the Saturday and get the extra few days with her sister, and so it was not until early on Monday morning that Amy found herself on the train and heading north, with a feeling of going home that she had not experienced for years. She had rung the house with her expected time of arrival and she knew there would be someone there at the station to meet her and drive her the four miles to Belmore House. She found her heart quaking a little at the thought that it might be Max. She had no idea how he was going to react to this return after so long.

From the year that she had gone to college, she had simply dropped her friends at Belmore House, and she knew they couldn't be expected to understand. They had all been so very good to her, actually loving her, and her desertion had been quite unforgivable. Very necessary, though, to Amy. At seventeen, she had developed the most awful crush on Max, and seeing him often had become a terrible embarrassment.

He had been twenty-eight, still treating her like a well loved relative until that last holiday, and she had to remove herself from the scene before he could find out. He had plenty of female companionship and certainly didn't need a starry-eyed teenager flinging herself at him. Luckily, at the end of that year she had gone to college, greatly relieved to discover that the feeling had been merely a crush, after years of affection and understanding between them. It was not the love of a lifetime. There had been a couple of boys at college who had pushed Max right out of her mind.

Even so, after making the break, she had never had enough nerve to start going to Northumberland again. She had lost touch with Bernice, but they had been such friends that she was unworried about that. No, it was Max who worried her. She had treated him very badly and maybe he would never forgive her. Amy suddenly smiled at such tragic and dramatic thoughts. He probably hadn't even noticed! He was very famous now. He was *the* Maxwell St Clair, his sculptures all over the world. She was very small fry in his important life.

As it turned out, it was Sebastian who met her, and she greeted him with great joy. He was five years younger than Max and he had never, in all the years that she had known him, been anything other than very quiet. It was sometimes impossible to think he was a brother to Max. The amused and quiet self-confidence that was part of the great charm that Max had was entirely missing in Sebastian. He had the family good looks, their superb manners and their great intelligence, but his shyness was so bad as to be an actual affliction. He was a solicitor in the nearby town, but how he ever managed to talk to clients had always been a mystery to Amy.

It must have taken some courage to come here to meet her. Amy pushed aside her own misgivings to put him at his ease at once.

'Sebastian!' She flew at him, giving him a great hug and allowing him no time to get worked up about this. It had always been necessary. As Max had once told her, 'If you want any action from Seb, you've got to force it out of him!' She forced him into ease, and his grateful brown eyes were sufficient reward.

'Well then, how are things at the homestead?' she asked brightly as they left the station and turned in the direction of Belmore House. 'I expect that Aunt Joan and Aunt Dorothy are knee-deep in plans that nobody will agree to?'

'Something like that,' he laughed. 'Bernice is there with the children, of course, but Jack can't get here until Friday.'

'I'm dying to see the children.' Amy felt another spasm of guilt. She had been asked to be bridesmaid when Bernice had married at twenty-three, but she had been too involved with her crush on Max to dare accept, and now there were two children, Simon who was five and Cheryl who was two. Amy had never even seen them.

'And how is Max?' she asked, in what she hoped was a hearty voice, sneakily trying to find out the lie of the land. If he was furious with her, then she had better prepare her defences.

'Oh, Max isn't here,' Sebastian told her in an offhand voice, 'though I expect he'll be here tomorrow. Glenys has been invited for dinner tomorrow night, so I imagine that Max will be back home in time to fetch her to the house.'

'Glenys?' Amy queried carefully. 'Er—this is the girlfriend, then?'

'Glenys Haworth,' Sebastian confirmed. 'Yes, I suppose she could be called the girlfriend—he always brings her home now, an unusual departure for Max.' From her eye corners, Amy could see that his face was a bit red; she had clearly embarrassed him with her chatter and she let the matter drop. It seemed, then, that Aunt Dorothy was

right. Max and marriage! According to the letter, Glenys
was sweet. Amy could just not see it. But then again, Max
was so powerful, vibrantly masculine, maybe he needed a
sweet little wife. Who could tell?

Amy need not have worried about her welcome. It was
ecstatic, and later she made her peace with Bernice.

'I'm sorry I didn't come to your wedding,' she said
softly, her blue eyes begging forgiveness. 'I—er—was a bit
odd at the time.'

'Amy darling, it was years ago! Anyway, we all get a
little odd at seventeen. I wasn't really surprised. I had
noticed that you were a bit strange. Hormones, I expect.'

'You're probably right,' laughed Amy, agreeing wholeheartedly. 'It's so good to be back, though. I can't wait to
see Max!' She knew that once again she was putting out
feelers, trying to find out if Max was furious with her, but
she still found nothing out at all.

'Oh, he'll be here tomorrow,' Bernice said drily. 'Glenys
is coming to dinner, and that will need Max to drag her
here and prevent her from fleeing—she's as bad as Seb.
Honestly, Amy, if Max didn't keep her right at his side,
she'd probably try to get up the chimney! And she's so
nice. It must be awful to be so painfully shy.'

'Oh dear,' sighed Amy. 'Do watch me, Bernice. You
know what I'm like for putting my foot in things!'

'She'll probably take to you and hang on to you like
glue!' said Bernice with a laugh. 'You're that sort of
person. The children have taken some getting to bed
tonight, having discovered a new and fascinating auntie.'

'Ah, well, I can't resist children,' Amy confided softly.
'According to some people, I never stopped being one

myself. I expect it's the job I do.'

'Maybe, but you're not all jolly hockey sticks, I'm relieved to see,' Bernice said, taking her arm and leading her off to dinner.

'Honestly?' begged Amy, happy to have her own opinion of herself confirmed. 'Describe me, please. I have this character crisis.'

'One word does it, darling,' Bernice assured her, giving her a hug. 'Quicksilver! You still make me feel like a great bumbling horse.'

'I *have* grown to a normal size!' protested Amy, laughing.

'Normal for you, dear!' Bernice stated with a glance at the vivid figure who walked beside her down the long, wide stairs. 'When we saw you on television at the games in Frankfurt, Max said, "Why, she's grown, she must be quite up to my chin now." You will be, too.'

'Did you see me?' Amy asked breathlessly. 'Did you see me win the hurdles?'

'Did we ever!' laughed Bernice. 'We threw our caps in the air, and believe it or not, when you went up to collect that medal, Dorothy and I were in tears. Max just said, "God, she's had her hair cut!" but he was proud as Punch.'

Next morning, in white shorts and bright red sports shirt, Amy went for her run before breakfast. It was, as Aunt Joan had predicted, glorious weather, and now, so early, there was that mist about the air that promised a hot and delightful day to follow. She was greatly at peace, back where she had always been happy, and her peace of mind spread through her body as she ran in the park, only one little trouble at the back of her mind. Today she would see

Max. She just couldn't bear it if he remonstrated with her, especially as she knew that even though she was at fault she would answer him back and spoil everything.

As she ran back up the drive, Bernice came out with the children and they came running to Amy instantly, forcing her to drop her pace and finally walk beside them.

'Oh, to have your stamina!' Bernice called when she was within earshot. 'Just looking at you tires me out!'

'You'll have to join me. You'll soon get fit,' Amy promised, but Bernice shook her head and laughed.

'Not me! I've just been trying to explain to these two what an athlete is, and even that made me feel tired!'

'Are you an athlete, Auntie Amy?' Simon wanted to know. 'Can you do cartwheels and somersaults and things like that?'

'Er—well, yes,' said Amy, knowing what was coming and frowning ferociously at a grinning Bernice.

'Do it! Do it!' Cheryl piped up, and Simon stood back to give her room, expecting instant action.

'Bernice!' Amy began warningly, but Bernice was already moving on to the big lawn, preparing to watch this unexpected treat, and one look into the excited eyes of the children was enough for Amy.

'Very well!' she sighed. 'On to the lawn then with Mummy. I can't do it here on this path.'

Never so obedient, they rushed off to sit with Bernice, and Amy pulled off her track shoes, leaving her white socks on her feet, deciding to take a chance on the damp grass. Anything to oblige!

Without warning, she kicked off from the edge of the lawn, hearing the screams of delight as she went from perfect cartwheels to forward somersaults, to handstands and back-flips, finishing with a sharp run that ended in a double somersault—a dazzling display of gymnastics that left Bernice and the children dazed. As she turned, there were four loud, slow, handclaps and she looked across to see Max standing at the bottom of the steps.

Her flushed face became hotter than ever, and she stood completely still as the children ran to him, calling excitedly. There was a curious little feeling inside her, a great and leaping happiness as the grey eyes regarded her steadily.

Max tilted his head on one side, looking at her as a slow, assessing smile curved his lips, and Amy could contain herself no longer. She raced across the lawn, her face alight with laughter as she threw herself at him and was caught in two powerful arms that hugged her close.

'Max! Max! It's so good to see you!'

Impulsively, she wound her arms around his neck and heard his soft laughter as he lifted her off her feet in a great and affectionate embrace.

'So you came home at last!' It was the first time she had heard that beloved voice in over five years and she didn't know whether to laugh or cry. What she did know was that she was happy, happy as she had not been for a very long time.

CHAPTER TWO

'How on earth did you do that?' Max was still holding her, looking down at her with those clear grey eyes, and Amy smiled up at him, fighting down a moment of unexpected panic.

'Do what?' She had forgotten how big he was, how powerful. Even now, when she was grown up, he towered over her, making her feel tiny and breakable.

'That dazzling display! I could have watched all day. It was over much too quickly.'

'Oh, I'm doing it all the time, after all,' she said with a quick, dismissive smile. 'It's no use telling the children at school to do something unless you can do it yourself, not in the gym anyway. They tend to think you're incapable if you don't demonstrate. Practice makes perfect!'

'I'm not sure whether you sound like a schoolmarm or my old nanny,' he remarked with an amused smile, his eyes flashing across her flushed face.

'Er—do you want to put me down, Max?' Amy said brightly, reminding him that he was still hugging her close.

'Not really, but I will if you insist.' He let her go, his smile broadening at her glowing confusion.

Amy stood back a trifle breathlessly as Bernice took the two excited children into the house for breakfast. 'I'd better get changed for breakfast, too,' she offered when Max simply went on looking at her.

'You look extremely exotic as you are. Go in like that.'

'I wouldn't dare! Your father's there this morning, and he's too important to be shocked. Anyway, I always shower after a run.' She turned away, but he caught her wrist and held her still.

'Hang on! I haven't seen you for more than five years! I'll begin to get the idea that you're avoiding me. Anyway,' he added, 'I have something to show you. Put your shoes on.'

'I will not!' She looked up at him with sparkling blue eyes. 'It would be extremely uncomfortable—my socks are wet from the grass. I'll come as I am.'

'You took a great chance performing like that at such a speed on damp grass!' said Max sternly, and she nodded in agreement.

'Children bring out the fool in me.'

'Almost anything does,' he countered, leading her off to the studio before she could get anything back at him.

It was just the same. The pieces were new but the feeling was there, the same smells, the same lighting, and Amy stopped in the doorway, sniffing the air like an animal seeking home.

Max watched her as she wandered down to the back, not expecting to see the small figurine but hopeful. It wasn't there.

'Oh, you sold my little statue!' she said, softly accusing, but he laughed, still standing by the door.

'Not a chance. That was mine. If you really want to know where it is, it's in my bedroom on the chest just behind the door. It's been there these many years.'

'You kept it?' Amy was terribly glad that he had. It had been so very special.

'Naturally! I made it for myself. One can afford these odd indulgences.' He came down to her, and moved along to a cupboard in the wall. 'What do you think of this?'

It was a small figure again, a nude in bronze, and Amy came slowly forward to look, no longer embarrassed by nudes. It was a girl, young and carefree, poised on one foot, her other leg thrown forward as if leaping some great obstacle with lightness and ease. The action was perfect. It could have been used as a teaching model to demonstrate the perfect hurdling position. Max turned it slowly and she saw the face.

'It's me, Max! How did you . . .?' She looked at him in some awe and he laughed at her surprise.

'No great mystery. After the games at Frankfurt, I wrote to the newspapers for photographs. I'm not unknown,' he added wryly, 'and they were happy to oblige. I modelled it from those. The face I knew.'

'I didn't look exactly like that,' Amy pointed out briskly. 'Much as it would be great to compete like that, one is expected to dress for the occasion!'

'It looks better like this!' he said firmly, eyeing it with satisfaction. 'This is as perfect as one could get. This is poetry in motion, just as you were on that lawn this morning. Care to pose for me while you're here? I could do a matching theme.'

'A forward somersault? How would you get me to hold the position? Did you bring me here to tell me you're going to give me this, Max?' she asked with a hopeful look at him, and he put the figure back in the cupboard very rapidly.

'No way!'

'Well, I don't much like the idea of that being in an exhibition!' she complained. 'The face is recognisable.'

'Well, I should just hope so! Anyway, what gave you the idea that I'd be showing it? Nobody has seen it but you. Lucky you came—I've been wanting to show it off for weeks.'

'But what are you going to do with it?'

'It goes in my room with the other one, naturally. It's mine, another act of self-indulgence.'

Amy wandered about, looking at the other things that were new to her, and Max walked beside her, commenting on first one and then the other.

'I saw your exhibition in London last autumn,' she murmured offhandedly. 'It was very good—no, it was wonderful.'

'I never saw you. Did you come on the first day?'

'No, the third, as a matter of fact. Clive and I went on the Saturday morning.'

'Ah, the boyfriend! Pity you didn't come on the first day when I was there. I could have given you my opinion of him.'

'Just how many more of those small bronzes are you intending to do for your private collection?' she asked suddenly, swinging to face him, her chin tilted as she met his grey eyes.

'Who knows? Whenever something about you strikes my mind. Maybe the next one will be when you're a bride, then when you're pregnant, then with your grandchildren. When I die, they'll be able to put them all in an exhibition and simply call them "Amy".'

'Don't talk like that! It gives me the creeps!' Amy looked at him accusingly. 'You're doing it on purpose—I know you, Max! Anyway, you'll run out of tops in your bedroom long before then.'

'I've bought a house,' he said, dumbfounding her. 'Next week the workmen are moving in to get the interior into good shape. I'll be able to display all my little treasures there.'

She was stunned at this sudden announcement, and stared at him, quite shocked. 'You're moving out of Belmore House?' And when he simply nodded, she added, 'So it's true. You are going to get married?'

'Possibly. In any case, don't you think it's time for me to move out of what you call the old homestead? I'm having a good, modern studio built, too, right beside it.'

'Well, I would never have believed it! Good job I didn't place any bets!' Amy turned to the door, quite stunned, and Max took her arm as he locked up, forcing her to wait.

'I'll take you to see the house. I would really value your opinion,' he said seriously, and she looked at him a little crossly, not quite sure how she felt about Max getting married, and clearly he was—he was just hedging.

'Whatever would you want my opinion for?'

'You're so damned outspoken,' he assured her sardonically. 'If it's not suitable, you'll tell me in no uncertain terms.'

'Why not ask the lady in question?' she said with a smile to match his.

'She likes surprises,' he confided quietly, 'and I like to indulge her.' So it was true!

He disappeared just before dinner and came back in

good time with Glenys Haworth, and Amy could tell as Max led her into the drawing-room that the girl was head over heels in love with him.

Bernice had not been exaggerating when she had said that Glenys hung on to Max and that he always had her under his wing. She was taller than Amy, slim to the point of being thin, but she had a lovely face, though a little too pale in Amy's opinion. Her hair was baby blonde, her pale blue eyes round and anxious. Actually, thought Amy, re-adjusting her perspective, anxious was a poor choice of description. Desperate was the word!

On seeing the whole family assembled for pre-dinner drinks, Glenys blushed to the roots of her hair, her eyes looking anywhere but at them all, and it was very clear that if Max had not had his arm draped around her shoulder she would have bolted. Amy was staggered, too, to see that Sebastian had also gone a bright and uncomfortable shade of pink.

She cast a sidelong glance at Bernice, who was sitting beside her, relaxed now that the children were asleep.

'What did I tell you?' muttered Bernice through almost closed lips. 'This is how the evening begins. After this, it gets worse!'

'I never thought to see two people like that in the same room at the same time!' Amy murmured. 'Surely it's a record of some sort?'

Bernice's splutter of laughter only served to draw Max's eyes to them with sharp and questioning disapproval, but Amy was not too worried about that. Glenys reacted with near terror, and Amy decided it was time to take a hand.

'Hello!' She stood up and walked lightly across the room. 'I'm Amy. Sorry I'll have to look up at you, but I haven't quite finished growing yet.' She shot out her hand and grasped the pale hand that Glenys offered tentatively. It was icy cold, shaking, and Amy's heart went out to her.

'What are you going to drink?' She tucked the hand in her arm and prized her away from Max, leading her then to the sideboard and pouring her a stiff gin and tonic. 'Now come and meet my aunt Joan—she's a terrible gossip! Anything you want to know about anybody you'll find out here!'

'You watch that tongue, Amy Tremaine!' her aunt laughed, but she made room for Glenys beside her and talked as only Aunt Joan could talk, spiritedly and at great length. Gradually, as the gin and Aunt Joan's barrage of chatter took effect, Amy had the satisfaction of seeing the painful red colour fade in the delicate, pretty face, and Glenys caught her eye, giving her a shy but grateful look, even managing a small smile when Amy raised her glass and said loudly,

'Bottoms up!'

She was surprised to receive another look of gratitude from Sebastian, his own colour returned to normal, and as Bernice left to have a quick glance at the children with a motherly anxiety, Max moved on to the settee to sit close to Amy.

'You're a good scout, Amy Tremaine,' he praised softly.

'Obviously this is my big day,' Amy conceded, with a glance at him from her eye corners. 'Praise is being heaped on my head.'

He looked at her head, his hand coming up to test the crisp, black, shining cloud of hair.

'Do you know, I was furious when you had your hair cut,' he told her. 'I was convinced for a while that it had

altered your facial expression, even your character. It was
quite a relief today to see that you were the same old
Amy—cheerful, cheeky and impetuous.'

'Good old me!' Amy said quietly, looking away from his
smiling grey eyes, faintly upset to hear him call her the
same old Amy, as if she were an old school chum. 'As to the
hair, it's mine. I have total tenure over the head.'

'Ah, I've annoyed you. I always was a little too
possessive about you. Remind me to ignore you and mind
my own business in future.' He started to get up and she
was instantly contrite, her hand coming to his arm.

'I'm sorry, Max, I didn't mean to be so bitchy. I've been
a little nervous about meeting you again, and when I get
nervous, I tend to go into battle.'

'I remember,' he laughed, sinking back beside her. 'So
what did you think I'd do to punish you for deserting me?
I never remember punishing you for anything.'

'I know.' She smiled to herself. 'You spoiled me.'

'I tried to,' he admitted, 'but with you, Amy, it just
wasn't possible. You've got a deep core of sweetness that's
quite incorruptible.'

For a moment, the smiling grey eyes met the brilliant
blue of her own, and she felt her face flush with pleasure.

'That may just be the nicest thing that anyone has ever
said to me,' she told him quietly, so very grateful that he
was still the Max she remembered.

'It even made you blush,' he countered. 'Now that's
something you *did* grow out of.'

Definitely, Amy thought as he left her and went to see if
Glenys needed to be rescued from Aunt Joan. When she
had reached the stage where the sight of him and the

thought of him had made her blush, she had taken to the hills fast.

'I saw you on television last year, when you won a medal at Frankfurt,' Glenys said at dinnertime, and all talk stopped at this unusual venture into sound by Glenys. Amy rushed into the breach before the attitude of the others, which was clearly astonishment, could penetrate to the shy and nervous girl.

'Yes, it was the high point of my life. The big moment,' Amy said with a smile.

'Is that what you do now, all the time? You look so full of life!' Glenys was leaning forward to speak, wanting to make conversation, and Amy could have hit Max when he chipped in.

'She's always been full of life,' he commented. 'There's a big furnace inside that small bundle.'

'You're so flattering to a girl,' she flashed at him, her brilliant blue eyes blazing before she decided to ignore him. 'No,' she answered, turning back to Glenys, 'competing in major games is a full-time job. I didn't have the time to devote to the training any more. I'm a Physical Education teacher.'

'She's Head of Department in a school in London,' Max added, and Amy turned on him again.

'I'm surprised you ever get anything done, what with your spying and all!'

'Hey! I was really proud of you. Head of Department, and you so young.'

'Well, as a matter of fact,' Amy laughed, 'nobody else would take it on. It's a rather tough school and there's a lot of chance to misbehave in the gym.'

'Do they?' Max asked aggressively.

'Oh no, not with Amy!' said Aunt Joan with a laugh, as Amy's eyebrows shot up at the very idea.

'Well, maybe not, after all,' he agreed with a slow smile.

Amy had a brisk go at him as they stood talking in the drawing-room after dinner. Glenys was talking to Sebastian and Max eyed them both with a satisfied look.

'Thanks to you, Amy, she's taken courage and is prepared to speak to someone. I didn't quite expect you'd take to her so readily.'

'Certain things touch my heart,' Amy assured him. 'Being as I am, I feel for people who are shy. Which reminds me to thank you for calling me a bundle. It quite went to my head!' She frowned up at him and he began to smile, that slow and secret smile that was so much a part of Max.

'You don't need flattery from me. You're quite beautiful and you know it.' His eyes slid over her petite figure, vibrantly alive in the silver-green dress that hugged her slender frame and flared around her calves. 'You have a lovely, glowing face, a perfect figure and the grace and poise of a ballet dancer. What else would you like me to say?'

'You could mention my brains,' she suggested lightly, beginning to feel hot and bothered for no good reason.

'I know they're there,' he assured her, 'but I happen to be an expert on the human form. In my job, it's necessary to know every muscle and bone in the body, every curve of the figure. Therefore, when I give my opinion, it counts.'

'Oh dear!' Amy gave a quick glance at him and looked rapidly away. 'It all sounds so clinical, but you needn't feel you have to boost my ego. I'm not a child any more.'

'I realise that,' Max said softly, turning away. 'You

stopped being a child when you were about seventeen. I noticed!'

He walked off to Glenys, and at that moment Amy needed someone to rescue her. Her own face was rose pink, and when she looked up Max was watching her with quizzical eyes, his dark eyebrows raised mockingly.

Amy went to bed, feeling secure in the same room she had always had at Belmore House. She needed the feeling of security. Her meeting with Max had quite shocked her, and left her with little of her normal breezy confidence. He seemed to have gone out of his way to remind her right from the first about exactly why she had fled from this house five years ago.

It had happened so unbelievably quickly, this new feeling she'd had for him. At seventeen, she had been so comfortable with Max, treating him like a big brother, then suddenly, in the course of one day, it had all changed. Memories that she had firmly squashed for five years came bounding to the surface of her mind, and she lay in bed, uneasily reliving them.

She was not sure now what it was that Max had done for her that had prompted her to give him a great hug and a kiss on the cheek, although she could remember doing it. She could remember rushing into the studio to thank him, running across to him and flinging her arms around his neck, standing on her toes to reach his great height.

She could even remember her words.

'Max, you're so wonderful! Oh, thank you, Max!'

It was his reaction to that small and uncomplicated kiss that had been the beginning of the end of her time here.

'If you're going to thank me, thank me properly,' he

had said softly, his arms locking round her and refusing to let go.

'I did!' She had looked startled, even then not at all aware of what was coming.

'Not really,' he had assured her with one of his slow smiles. 'I think that if you're going to kiss someone, especially me, you should do it wholeheartedly, like this!'

Now he was holding her with only one arm, a strong arm like iron, that held her to him with no offer of escape—not that she thought of escaping, not then. His other hand came to her long, black hair, his fingers spearing through it, capturing her head as his lips covered hers for the first time in a kiss that took her breath away and set her heart hammering wildly.

When he reluctantly lifted his head, she could not utter a sound. Her eyes were brilliantly blue in her pale face as she stared up at him in a shocked silence.

'Max?' she managed to say, as he simply looked down at her, watching her reaction. At her questioning and shaken look he smiled and stroked her face, still not freeing her from his tight embrace.

'Amy?' His eyes were slightly derisive, a look she had never seen before on him, and it confused her even more.

'Why—why did you—you kiss me?'

'Why not?' he countered. 'Maybe I wanted bigger and better thanks, or maybe I'm no longer sure that I want to be such a comfortable figure in your airy life.'

'But—but I've always loved you, Max! I look forward to seeing you. I—I need you like . . .'

'Like an old well-known dog, like a security blanket?' he asked wryly. 'Step one in growing up, poppet: don't take anyone at their face value.'

And she couldn't after that. The kiss had awakened
something in her that she could not control. Other kisses
had left her with no feeling at all, but they had been kisses
given to her briefly by boys she knew, and few of them at
that. This was different. It was a kiss from a man to a
woman, and she wanted more.

She found herself watching Max differently, watching
him all the time, and she found too that his eyes were not
smiling in the same way when he looked at her. She ran! It
was the only thing to do, because she could not come to
terms with the new and devastating feelings that were
growing inside.

She sighed and turned over, drifting off to sleep. It had
all been a long time ago, when she was still a child in her
body and mind. She was no longer so vulnerable.
Anyway, Max had only been teasing; he was getting
married, after all.

Next morning, Max was already in the studio when
Amy came down to breakfast, and she abandoned her
usual run goodnaturedly when the children begged to be
taken for a walk. Bernice had looked quite sick at the idea,
and Amy decided to take them off her hands for half an
hour or so. The idea was received with great enthusiasm
by the children, who demanded to be taken 'on the hill', a
high rise of land behind the house. Bernice agreed to
accompany them as far as the front steps and no further.

Max was just coming into the house, and he looked at
Amy in her jeans and shirt.

'No run? I expected to see you racing back in when I got
up at seven. I wonder if you're a fraud?'

'She's taken on an act of supreme self-sacrifice,' Bernice
told him. 'She's taking the children on the hill. All the

running she needs will be provided there.'

'I think I can catch these two,' Amy said with a laugh, but Bernice and Max smiled at each other secretly.

'They run in opposite directions,' said Max with a certainty of experience. 'I'll come with you.'

'I'm an expert on children!' protested Amy.

'Not the fast-moving miniature variety!' Max said firmly. 'I'll come!'

'Who invited him?' Amy enquired of the sunny sky, but he came anyway, falling into step beside her, taking Cheryl on his back after a very short while, leaving Amy free to chase Simon, who was as fast on his feet and as sinuous as a little fieldmouse.

'I see what you mean,' she conceded breathlessly when she had captured Simon for the third time. 'I can now understand Bernice's horror at the mention of a walk. It's a good thing you're here.'

'She wants me, after all!' Max murmured to Cheryl as she clung to his neck.

'Everybody wants Uncle Max,' Simon stated determinedly, and Amy spluttered with laughter.

'Lord, what a reputation!' she murmured in a voice just loud enough for Max to hear, her eyes sparkling with fun as he gave her an exaggerated frown.

It was lovely on the hill, breezy and sunny, and Amy flung herself on to the grass as the children scrambled in the bushes and played hide and seek with each other.

Max stretched out beside her, resting on his elbows, looking down at the house that now seemed quite a distance away.

'How long are you staying?' he asked.

'I've offended you already?' Amy enquired with mild

astonishment, and he laughed softly.

'You know I don't mean that. We've missed you, Amy. You became a necessary part of our lives.' He was serious, and she didn't want that for some reason, but the jocularity left her voice.

'I have to get back at the weekend. I have duties at school next week.'

'It's the long summer holiday!' Max protested. 'Stay for the whole time.'

'There's a match arranged for next week. I've got to be there to take the girls.' She sat up, crossing her legs, her arms across her knees. 'Don't tempt me too much, though. It's so good to be back here.'

'Why did you stay away so long?' Max asked quietly, and she fought hard to keep an easy-sounding voice.

'Oh, college and then work. You get drawn into a different life-style. Sport took up a lot of my time. When I was competing, I had to train seriously every single day. Other things just grow sort of—distant.'

'Now that you're back here, it feels as if you've never been away,' he said softly, and she looked across at him, smiling.

'I know, it's wonderful!'

'Is it lunch time?' Simon wanted to know. 'Elevenses?' he enquired further, when the answer was negative.

'Collect Cheryl and we'll go back, then,' said Max, standing and reaching out a hand to help Amy, as Simon raced off for his sister.

'How exhausting they must be!' Amy commented, watching them. 'Why did I offer to take on this torture?'

'Good practice for when you have children of your own,' he assured her with a slow smile.

'No horror stories, please,' said Amy with a shudder. 'Why should I even contemplate such a disastrous event?' But his smile merely grew.

'With you, Amy, it's inevitable. You were born to be someone's wife and have their children.'

'I'm a modern, freewheeling games-person!' Amy asserted, looking up into two smiling grey eyes.

'For now. The time will come, though.' She suddenly found her eyes locked with his, his face closer than she had imagined, her heart racing as if she had just run up the hill. He slowly cupped her face in his hands and, without warning, kissed her, his lips lightly exploring hers.

'Why did you do that?' she whispered, still trapped by his strong hands, although he had raised his head.

'Curiosity,' he murmured, his face still close to hers. 'I'm still curious.'

'Are you kissing Auntie Amy, Uncle Max?' Simon asked with a great deal of interest as he ran up.

'Certainly not!' Max lied smoothly, still holding her face. 'She has something in her eye.'

'What is it?' Simon wanted to know.

'The light of battle!' muttered Amy in a low voice as Max released her, but all she heard was his soft and mocking laughter as he scooped up Cheryl and followed down the hill.

'Go easy!' she called to Simon as he frolicked off on the steep descent. 'Don't start something you can't stop!'

'That's good advice,' laughed Max as he walked behind her. 'I'll make a note of that and put it up in my bedroom, just to remind me.'

Amy was glad that he couldn't see her face. His kiss had been gentle, a mere brushing of his lips, but her own lips still tingled with a strange thrill, and a dangerous spark was trying to fan itself to life inside her. She wasn't going to let him get to her again. She loved it here. This time, Max was not going to make her run!

There was a visitor having coffee with her aunts as they got back, and he was introduced to Amy as Douglas Heaton, son of the local vet. It appeared he was following in his father's footsteps, and was already as popular as his father.

'Oh, I remember your father very well,' Amy said as she shook hands. 'Many's the time he took me on his rounds. I suppose I got in his way terribly, but it was great fun, especially when the bull at one farm chased me. He swore then that he'd never take me out with him again, but he did!'

'He remembers you too, Miss Tremaine,' Douglas Heaton laughed. 'He sends his regards and his admiration at your win at Frankfurt. I'm to tell you that now he knows how you managed to get away from the bull.'

'Oh dear! I think almost everyone saw me win at Frankfurt,' smiled Amy. 'It really is very gratifying, the only time I'll ever be famous. I'd love to see your father again.'

'Come up to the house,' he said quickly. 'We'd love it. Have tea with us one day while you're here.'

'Oh, thank you. I'd like that.'

He was a very pleasant man, Amy thought. Good-looking too, with the easy, well-mannered grace that had always been so much a part of his father.

'I can't think why I don't know you,' she mused. 'It's odd that, in all my time coming here, I never met you once.'

'You did, Miss Tremaine,' he said wryly. 'You must

have been about sixteen at the time, and I was home from university. It was at the sheepdog trials. I remember I was very impressed by you, but you were hanging on to Max like glue. I gave him best. He was awfully strong-looking!'

He turned to her aunt Dorothy.

'Well, Mrs St Clair, I suppose I'd better give Smithers the once-over? He looked ruefully amused. 'I can never understand why you called a perfectly respectable cat by that name.'

'She didn't,' Max assured him, his arm coming casually around Amy's slender shoulders. 'Amy did that. Dorothy was utterly opposed to it, but Amy continued to call him Smithers until he answered to that only. Short of giving the cat a nervous breakdown, there was nothing to do but surrender.'

'Well, if it was your idea, Miss Tremaine, then it suits him,' Douglas Heaton said gallantly.

'I wish you'd call me Amy,' she said with a grimace. 'Miss Tremaine makes me feel so old, and I get it all the time at school. Is Smithers all right?' she added a little anxiously, remembering that she had not seen the old but cunning cat since she had come.

It was very hard to be casual with Max's arm around her shoulders. She tried to surreptitiously ease away, but he tightened his grip with the same casual ease he had shown when he had first put his arm there.

'For a cat of his age, in the pink!' she was assured. She was greatly relieved when everyone else came in for coffee and Max was obliged to remove his arm. She didn't like it, it was much too warming.

'Of course, you're coming to the trials tomorrow?' asked Douglas in a determined voice when they were all seated.

'There'll be the usual fair there, and the home-produce stalls—all the money goes to the local charities.'

'I had no idea it was tomorrow!' Amy exclaimed with an accusing look at her aunt Dorothy.

'My dear, I quite forgot to tell you, but you would have been taken there, anyway. We're all going, with the exception of Max, of course!'

'I'm going,' said Max, leaning back beside Amy on the settee. 'I'm going to take Amy on the roundabout.'

'I'll be sick!' Amy said promptly, and he looked across at her with laughing grey eyes.'

'All right then, I'll push you on the swings.'

There was a look in his eyes that set her heart racing, and he just kept right on looking at her; she could feel it even though she talked spiritedly to Douglas Heaton and her aunts. She wondered why he was doing it. Maybe Glenys had good reason to be nervous and anxious!

Douglas stayed for ages, and Amy was highly amused at the interest he took in her. He really was very nice, and he acted as if she had arranged to see him alone when she assured him that nothing would keep her from the trials tomorrow.

'Now, there's a young man who's very interested in our Amy!' Bernice remarked with a wicked grin, as he finally drove away from the house.

'He's an improvement on Clive,' Aunt Joan assured Bernice, and Amy gave a yelp of outrage.

'Unfair! You don't know Clive at all, Aunt Joan!'

'God is good to me,' her aunt countered darkly. 'Stay here longer and get to know that nice young man.'

Amy was shaken with laughter. Her aunt was always trying to find her a 'nice young man'. Max was quiet and interested but, to Amy's relief, Aunt Joan let the matter drop and Bernice began a long and involved tale about the children, capturing Amy then to take her upstairs and show her a new dress that required an outside opinion. By dinner time, Max had returned to normal, and all his energies, all his attention, were directed towards Glenys, who was there again.

CHAPTER THREE

THE NEXT day, Thursday, was half-closing day in the small market town, so there was a very big turn-out for the local show and sheepdog trials. Max did not go, after all, when the rest of them left Belmore House—in fact, he was nowhere to be seen, and Amy was annoyed with herself to feel disappointed. He always had been there before; he was part of the sunny memories of this annual outing.

Even so, she enjoyed it immensely. Douglas Heaton took her under his wing at once, monopolising her time and rather skilfully cutting out the rest of the family, to Bernice's amusement. There was a good breeze here, high on the hills that overlooked the town, and Amy stood by the fence, her foot on the bottom bar, her arms folded comfortably on the top bar, Douglas beside her as she watched the trials, anxiously cheering on her favourite, a small collie bitch.

'Such enthusiasm! You do get worked up about it!' Douglas laughed, looking down at her with a grin, and she tossed her head, her hair black and shining in the sunlight.

'We who are small must support each other!' she said, with smiling determination.

'She'll not win, she doesn't have the experience,' Douglas told her with the certainty of inside knowledge. 'That's going to be the champion, over there.' His hand came to her shoulder and he bent his head towards her as he pointed out the other dog. Max arrived at that moment, strolling across with Glenys, his eyes intently on

Amy and the young vet.

'Oh, hello!' Amy smiled brightly at Max, but got, to her surprise, a look of silent and deep consideration that made her wonder very rapidly if she had done something wrong. She turned her smile on Glenys instead. Max was *not* going to be allowed to spoil her day.

'You're just in time for the big event, Glenys!' she said.

When Glenys looked surprised, Douglas laughed delightedly. 'She's talking about the rather grand picnic lunch that Mrs St Clair always brings here for the family,' he explained. 'She's been going on about it all morning. I've heard of little else. Anyone would think she was only interested in food!'

'I *am* interested in food!' Amy protested, giving him the sort of cheerful push that showed how well they had become acquainted in such a short time. 'I use bags of energy!'

'You're so beautifully neat, it's really hard to believe that you have any appetite at all,' Douglas said admiringly, and Max raised one dark eyebrow, his grey eyes coolly derisive as he looked at Amy.

'Oh, look—Sebastian has arrived!' Glenys said, to Amy's utter astonishment. 'I'll just nip over and have a word with him.' She did, and Amy felt quite stunned. The idea of Glenys nipping across to have a word with anyone at all just refused to settle evenly in her mind. Her startled eyes met Max's and he took her arm in a hard grip.

'Lunch time!' he said decisively. 'This part of the show is over.'

He nodded politely to a clearly disappointed Douglas, and guided Amy off, none too gently.

'Oh, isn't Douglas invited to lunch with us?' she asked

with a deliberately wistful look, and Max simply tightened his hold.

'Not unless your aunt Dorothy has invited him,' he said grimly. 'This is a family gathering.'

'Glenys is here!' she said, being deliberately provocative.

'Need I explain that Glenys is in an entirely different category?'

'Well, I've been with Douglas for the entire morning. Doesn't that make him a bit special?' Amy shot him a brilliant glance and he stopped, looking down at her with punishing intensity until her cheeks flushed.

'Clearly, he thinks so. He doesn't quite yet know the extent of the fire that burns inside that small frame. He even thinks you're too delicate to eat. Maybe he should be invited to see you get those perfect little teeth into the beef!'

'You make me feel like a voracious carnivore!' she protested.

'But you're so very *neat*, Amy. Douglas said so!' He was so sardonic, so unlike Max, that her face clouded.

'I think you're going to spoil my day,' she accused softly, and to her relief the smile came back into his eyes.

'Not unless you provoke me, sweet. I look forward to this day too, now that you've come back home.'

'Well, you'll have Glenys to look after this time,' Amy said brightly. 'You can safely leave me to my own devices.'

'I've never felt like leaving you to your own devices,' Max said quietly. 'As to Glenys, look how well she gets on with Seb. With a bit of luck, she'll stick with him and I can stay with you.'

'Whatever can you mean?' Amy asked rather wildly. 'She expects you to be with her—I mean, she clearly can't manage without you. I can cope with almost anything!'

'Almost!' he agreed, with a slow look at her flushed face. 'Then again, Glenys is here permanently. You'll race off soon, out of my life. Isn't it natural that I should want to see as much of you as possible?'

Amy said nothing. She had no idea what had come over her. She was far too aware that Max stood close to her. He was making her skin tingle. She had long ago grown out of the crush she had had on him, so what was the matter with her now?

The picnic lived up to all expectations, but somehow Amy's appetite was quite gone. Glenys talked more than she did. Out of the atmosphere of the house, Glenys seemed to be much more easygoing, and Sebastian, too, blossomed in the relaxed surroundings, spending much of his time keeping Glenys entertained.

'I hope that my remarks about your small and perfect teeth didn't put you off lunch,' Max whispered in her ear. He was deliberately sitting close to her, and she was astonished that the rest of the family hadn't noticed, but of course, they had nothing to feel guilty about. She was the one with the guilt, beginning to feel so odd about Max, with his future wife sitting there so innocently unaware of this situation.

'I—I suddenly find I'm not really hungry!' She tried to be sharp and forbidding, but it never worked with Max as it worked with other people.

'Try this, it's really good,' He popped a piece of pie into her mouth that he had broken off from his and, short of making a scene, she was forced to eat it, blushing furiously as his eyes watched her lips all the time.

'Delicious!' he said seductively, adding with a sardonic

smile, 'Wasn't it?' Amy was glad when the whole thing was over.

'Let's walk round.' He took her arm firmly and she had no real choice. Glenys was deep in conversation with Sebastian. Bernice had taken the children to the swings, and her aunts were greeting old friends who had come up to talk.

From then on she seemed to be gushing over everything, things that did not particularly interest her, like home-made pickles, and it was only Max's soft laughter that finally brought her to a breathless halt.

'Take it easy! You'll never stay the course at this rate,' he warned, turning her towards him. He wound a finger around a piece of her hair, his eyes amused and warm, but she jerked her head away.

'Let's not make an exhibition of ourselves!' she said a trifle sharply, and his eyes narrowed thoughtfully.

'So you *do* find me too possessive!'

'I—I'm sorry, Max, I really don't know what's come over me,' she apologised, and he took her hand, drawing it through his arm.

'Never mind, poppet. As a treat, I'll let you see my new house tomorrow.'

'I don't think that's much of a treat,' she shrugged, looking at him sideways, and he tightened her to his side, never even looking at her.

'But I need you to see it, Amy. I need your advice, and I have this awful feeling I should always have my own way, especially with you. It comes from having fashioned you in permanent materials, I expect. I just have this odd feeling that I've created you.'

'That's a pretty scary thing to say!' gasped Amy, swinging to face him.

'Oh, I don't know,' mused Max, his eyes on her startled face. 'I'm quite prepared to take the responsibility.'

Next morning, when Amy presented herself for breakfast, Max eyed her determinedly.

'All set to go?'

'I'm not going back to London until Sunday,' she told him with a pert look. 'Or did I really, finally, offend you?' She was determined to get a grip on this situation.

'I'm talking about my house and your immediate inspection of it. Let's have no hedging!' He gave her a stern look as he pushed the toast across to her. 'I'm ready to leave as soon as you've refuelled.'

'You actually meant it, Max? I really don't see what I can do to set your mind at rest about the purchase of a dwelling for your wife. She'll really have to see it herself!'

'You never have set my mind at rest about anything, as I recall,' he mused with a considering look that told her he was flicking through some mental file. 'From time to time, though, you've given me pause for thought. I want your honest and forthright opinion, and I'm sure I'll get it!'

'Well, you'll surely have asked for it!' countered Amy, stifling a small and niggling irritation at the thought of ironing out difficulties for Glenys and now, to her astonishment, a small but definite flicker of unease at being alone with Max.

It was a lovely morning, however, just the day for a drive, and later, sitting by Max in his car, she relaxed into the old, old feeling. The sun was shining, the wind was in her hair and Max was the same comfortable, vaguely exciting man that he had always been. He still had that small, secret smile that edged around his mouth, the handsome face still looked with a faintly sardonic amusement at the world, and she realised that there was nowhere else she would rather be than beside him. Her peculiar fears of yesterday had quite gone.

'Are you happy?' he asked, with a sidelong look at her when she made a small, contented sound.

'Perfectly!' She leaned back and closed her eyes, soaking in the morning sun.

'Care to tell me why?'

'I honestly don't know. Does there have to be a reason?' Amy opened one eye and peered at him. 'Happiness just bubbles up inside you—well, it does with me.'

'All the time?'

'I can see I'm going to have problems with you today,' Amy sighed, sitting up and looking around. 'What is this philosophical mood, pray?'

'I only asked!' Max looked comically grieved and she laughed, impulsively winding her arm through his, her happiness truly bubbling over.

'All right then—no, I'm not always happy. I do have problems, just like everyone else. Very rarely but very definitely. They are not, however, very real, and when I'm here, sitting with you, back in this place, my little problems suddenly seem quite silly. Does that answer your question?'

'Yes, I think it probably does,' he said quietly, his secret smile growing. 'It also confirms my belief that you haven't changed at all.'

'I know,' she sighed. 'I'm still small.'

'Petite!' Max corrected firmly, swinging the car off the main road and down a tree-shaded side road. 'You're nicely up to my chin, and that's a good height to be!'

'I honestly never noticed you doing any measuring!' she countered with wide and mockingly astonished blue eyes.

'An estimation. As I told you, I'm good at that sort of thing. Here's the house.' He suddenly swung into an overgrown driveway and the house in question was soon there for her to see. It was old, red brick, long and pleasing to the eye.

'A country mansion, modest but genuine!' Amy pronounced. 'From here, I give it full marks.' She skipped lightly out of the car as Max stopped at the door and immediately began an external inspection.

'There's been, at one time, a very beautiful garden here,' she announced firmly. 'Something wants doing about that right away. Then, when the house is ready, the garden will be ready at the same time.' She walked around the outside, her eyes critically scanning the brickwork.

'Repointed, new window frames, all completed,' Max assured her, taking her arm.

'Guttering?'

'Finished!' He turned her firmly to the front door. 'I want a woman's view of the interior, which isn't yet started,' he said determinedly. 'A builder I do not need. I already pay one!'

'I don't want to be charged later on with negligence!' Amy protested. 'In any case, my fees are very small.'

Inside the front door, though, her flippancy left her. Some houses had a soul of their own, and this was one of them. It was happy here. Joy had been known in this house, and it seemed to welcome her with a warmth that was tangible.

'It's silenced you,' Max said softly. 'I've never been able to do that. Do you hate it, then?'

'It's lovely, Max,' Amy assured him with a softness of her own. 'I could give my opinion of this house without even taking one more step inside.' She turned glowing blue eyes on him, looking up into his still face. 'Thank you for bringing me, for allowing me to see it.'

He reached out and touched her hair. 'You don't usually go over the top about anything.'

'Oh, I do!' she protested seriously. 'Sometimes I feel very deeply!'

'Come on!' He took her arm again and led her into the sunny drawing-room. Amy was silent, her eyes darting everywhere, knowing full well that Max was highly amused, but not being able to contain her enthusiasm for the place.

It was more than enthusiasm, she realised with a swift pang of guilt. It was jealousy! She wanted this house. She wanted to plan it with Max, to buy the furniture and arrange it, to determine the décor, to choose the pictures.

She fell silent, only forcing herself to smile brightly when she discovered that he was watching her with deep interest.

'It's perfect!' she announced with a glittering smile. 'I'm sure that Glenys will love it.'

'I'm glad you think so. I knew I could rely on you for an opinion. Let's look at the other rooms.'

He finally led her back to the hall, but Amy had a strange reluctance to leave this place, a tearful desire to cling and refuse to go out again into the sunlight of the garden.

'Can't we go upstairs?' she asked.

'I'm not too keen on you going up there,' Max confessed steadily. 'The stairs are a bit dangerous—the whole flight will have to come out. Still,' he added, seeing her disappointment, 'if you can be very careful, I expect we could risk it. The next to the bottom step, though, is rotten, so avoid it!'

She did, going up with great care and wishing, when she had arrived, that she had not pressed the point. It was a house filled with love, and it was making her more unhappy by the minute. She felt possessive about this house, and to her astonishment the possessiveness was rapidly growing to include Max!

'What does Glenys do for a living?' she asked idly, wandering around, with no further comments to make in case she gave herself away.

'She's a secretary, at the firm where Sebastian works. That's how I met her.'

'She works for Sebastian?' Amy's astonishment was glaringly obvious, and he laughed.

'No, for Townsend, the senior partner.'

'How awful! He's been dead for years—no wonder she's so nervous!'

'What are you talking about? He's very much alive. He's only sixty!'

'He's been parchment and dust since I was in my teens,' Amy assured him. 'Poor Glenys!'

'She's quite comfortable with him. He presents no undue challenge.'

'Ah, well . . .' Amy suddenly stopped. She was about to say that Max was challenge enough for any woman, but she thought better of it. 'Shall we be going now?' She turned to the door and started down the stairs, leaving Max staring at her straight and slender back with thoughtful eyes. She moved gracefully, her head poised like a dancer, every movement unknowingly perfect—but she had forgotten the step Max had warned her of.

Suddenly her foot seemed to give way beneath her, and there was a sound of tearing wood. Even though her steps were light, her left foot went through the step and became firmly lodged in the splintered wood.

'Max!' Her sharp cry alerted him and he moved swiftly out on to the passage, then saw her bent over, clutching the banister, clearly in pain.

'Don't try to move!' He came down the steps fast, careless of safety, and took her weight, easing her into his arms as he crouched beside her, lessening the strain on her ankle.

'I've gone through!' She tried to joke about it, but her face showed the pain she felt and he never smiled.

'Keep still. Let's see how we can free you.' He lowered her on to the next step and began a gentle inspection of the trapped ankle. 'Just relax, Amy, and I'll pull the wood away. When I tell you, ease your foot out and on to the step.'

They managed it but, by the time the foot was free, Amy was white with pain and shock, and Max pulled her back into his arms.

'God, I must have been mad to bring you here! I know you can get into trouble without any kind of help.' His voice was self-accusatory, and Amy pulled herself together.

'It's only a sprain, for heaven's sake! I'll be as good as new tomorrow. I've got to be—I'm going back to London.'

'I doubt that,' he said tightly, inspecting the now swelling ankle. 'Come on, we'll get you over to the hospital!'

He swung her up into two strong arms and she could tell he never even felt her weight at all. It made her a little dizzy, and she didn't know why. Maybe it was the shock, or maybe it was that she had not been in Max's arms for so very long.

'It's only a sprain, Max,' she protested. 'There's

absolutely no need whatever to cart me off to hospital. I can tell it's a sprain—I did anatomy and physiology at college!'

'I'm impressed but not convinced. An X-ray will convince me.' Max carried her to the car and then went back to lock up the house. 'Brave little soul, aren't you? Not one tear.'

'I've had plenty of falls in my time,' said Amy nonchalantly, gritting her teeth and turning her head so that he would not see the pain on her face.

'Hang on, darling. We'll be there in no time,' he promised softly, and she came to agitated life.

'You've no business to call me that! You're getting married soon!' she accused with more heat than kindness, but he only laughed softly, ignoring her anger.

'It makes no difference to us! Anyway, you're still a baby, aren't you?'

'Clive doesn't think so!' she snapped. 'Don't mistake smallness of stature for immaturity!'

'How you do go on,' he said amiably. 'I expect it's the pain. Shock can do terrible things to people.'

It *was* a sprain. Amy was quite gleeful about her diagnosis and highly amused to be wheeled back to the waiting-room at the local hospital in a new and rather splendid wheelchair.

'I'll take her,' Max said firmly when the nurse had brought her down the corridor and, dismissing the chair, he lifted her again into his arms.

'I fancied being wheeled to the car!' Amy protested. 'I could borrow that chair if I wanted to. I could have it for a week!'

'You don't need it!' Max said determinedly, nodding to the laughing nurse who opened the door for them. 'On foot, you're a menace; mechanised, you could do untold damage. You don't need drama, you carry your own around with you!'

'And how, pray, am I expected to get around the house? I have, this minute, been told to rest the foot!'

'One roller-skate? A pogo stick?' Max suggested ironically. 'Better still, stay in bed!'

'Actually,' said Amy, when he had settled her in the car and they were once again on their way, 'it's not at all amusing. I have a team to take across London, and I promised to be there.'

'Well, clearly you can't be. Get Clive to take them.' Max looked a little grim, but she ignored that.

'Clive takes maths, he wouldn't know what to do with a whistle. I could try Kitty, though,' she added thoughtfully. 'I did do her the favour of suggesting to Clive that he take her to the Albert Hall instead of me. She likes him very much. So she owes me one.'

'You seem to live a strange and disordered life,' Max remarked in astonishment. 'Trading your boyfriend for a favour! Why didn't you go to the Albert Hall yourself?'

'I was coming here,' Amy reminded him. 'I had to do some pretty fast talking to get out of the promise I'd made to Clive.'

'You preferred to come here, Amy?' he asked softly, but she wasn't falling into that trap.

'Aunt Joan blackmailed me! Anyway,' she added truthfully, 'I wanted to come back, if only to make my peace with Bernice and Seb. Of course, there was you.'

'Of course!' he laughed. 'I can quite see your dilemma. Phone Kitty, by all means, and see if she'll be willing. As this is the long summer holiday, you can stay for weeks.'

'Life exists beyond Northumberland!' Amy reminded

him tartly, but secretly she was glad. It was worth a sprained ankle any day to prolong her stay with Max.

The fuss that Amy had to endure was astonishing. It seemed that Max deliberately carried her into the house and deposited her on the settee in the drawing-room to enable Aunt Joan and Aunt Dorothy to hover over her to their hearts' content. Securely trapped, she could do nothing, and Max simply disappeared. Bernice's attitude was more down-to-earth.

'Good, now you can't go back!' she said with a certain wicked satisfaction, and the children seemed to be equally delighted. Max's father was by now back in London dealing with the business of the state, no doubt, and after an hour of the undivided attention of most of the household, Amy heartily wished that she was with him.

Max rescued her after a while, but only, she felt, because he came in unexpectedly and saw her attempts to hobble across the room when at last the others had gone off for a minute and she had peace.

'Bed!' he said with an expression that she knew well. 'I might have known you weren't to be trusted!'

'And what am I supposed to do in bed?' Amy asked crossly. 'I simply don't have the ability to lie and contemplate the ceiling.'

'I'll get Bernice to bring you a selection of books,' he promised, scooping her up and making for the hall. 'Meanwhile, I'll get this foot to bed, where it may get some chance to rest.'

'I resent your possessive attitude towards my foot!' Amy told him. 'The foot's mine, so I feel I should have some say in the matter. Had you permitted the bringing of the chair I wouldn't now be in your power!'

'Imagine, if you will, the problems of wheeling yourself down this great flight of stairs,' Max said reasonably, stopping in the hall to gaze into her flushed face. 'The mind refuses to take in difficulties of such magnitude. The obvious solution would be for me to leave the chair upstairs and carry you down. As I would then have to perform the same service for the chair, I decided the moment I saw it that it should remain in the more sterile surroundings of the hospital!'

'I give in!' Amy sighed dramatically, and curled up more comfortably against his chest. It wasn't at all difficult to endure this. She might as well make the most of it, because, when he was married, her days were over. It was pleasant, the way he accepted her soft movement and tightened her against him. She couldn't help feeling safe with Max.

Of course, she was allowed down for dinner, a stool being found to take the weight of her foot, which by now was throbbing painfully, and she was thankful that Glenys was not there tonight. She wasn't feeling up to doing her bit in that direction and, without the presence of a person who was not yet a member of the family, Sebastian lost much of his tight embarrassment and shyness and simply went out of his way to take care of her, plying her with food and drink and being extremely solicitous.

Amy could see that trouble of this sort brought out the best in him, and wondered how it could be turned to his advantage. For the moment, though, she couldn't think of a way, short of spraining the ankle of any girl he might be interested in.

Max, though, was not too delighted.

'Only one glass of wine for Amy, Sebastian!' he said in a

commanding tone that brought a resentful flush to his brother's face. 'Chances are that she may need pain-killers for that foot tonight, and the less she has to drink, the better.'

'I suppose I should have thought of that,' Sebastian admitted with a muted annoyance. 'It's such a great pleasure to get the chance to care for Amy, that I quite overlooked it!'

'I'd much rather go to bed roaring drunk than take pain-killers,' Amy said quickly, seeing the light of battle in both their eyes and not understanding it one little bit.

'You're not getting the chance to decide!' Max told her with an annoyance that was utterly new for him. 'And, speaking of bed, it's time you were back there soon. Let me know when you're ready and I'll carry you up—unless Seb would like to take on the task?'

'Any time!' said Sebastian, his face going from white to red and back again. Amy made to move from the table before his embarrassment became more acute. The rest of the family were as stunned as she was herself, and it was Bernice who helped her into the drawing-room for coffee.

When she did make a move for bed, however, Max stood and lifted her without a word, to make his way upstairs with his bewildered and slightly resentful burden.

'Do you know what you've done?' she muttered as soon as the door was closed behind them. 'You've put Sebastian back about five years, and you've made me feel utterly stupid and troublesome!'

'Possibly. Sometimes I feel bad-tempered just like everyone else.' He managed an elegant shrug of his shoulders even as he carried her up the stairs, and she glared up at him.

'Next time, then, take it out on me! I can take it, Sebastian can't.'

'I'll try to remember,' said Max shortly, lowering her to her bed and glancing round to see that she had her nightie to hand. 'Anything else I can do for you?'

'No, thank you. Goodnight!' Amy said sharply, her eyes resentfully on him. She knew perfectly well why he was so bad-tempered. Glenys had not been there tonight, and Bernice had said that Glenys had been called away unexpectedly to visit a sick cousin in Durham. Clearly, he could not manange to get along for even one day without a sight of her.

He looked at her expressionlessly and she stared back in like manner. His smile was missing. It was not even in his eyes, and a great surge of tenderness suddenly swept over her. Who was she to judge Max? He had taken care of her for years when she had come here, and she knew that he also took care of Seb, going out of his way to make life smooth for him.

'I forgive you all your sins, large and small,' she offered, her smile winging out to him. 'Thank you for taking care of me and—and . . .'

'How can I not?' he said softly, his eyes warming. 'After all, it's a habit. Goodnight, Amy.'

He smiled at her from the doorway, and she was glad that she had made her peace with him.

Taking a sprained foot lightly was not a very good idea, Amy decided when, at midnight, she was still restless with pain. At home, she would have known exactly where the pain-killers were, but here she had no idea where to look.

Carefully she got out of bed, and finally made it to her bathroom to search, but there was nothing there to help. It seemed she must go down the stairs, whether she wanted to or not.

She managed to get the top of the stairs by hopping and sliding along the wall, making more noise than she had intended, but the stairs themselves proved to be relatively easy. She simply sat at the top and lowered herself down one step at a time. To any casual observer, she realised, she would have looked an utter fool. Her face was stiff with concentration and her mode of descent was anything but graceful.

She found the whole thing highly amusing, even though the pain was really bad, and her stiff face relaxed as she began to laugh softly, her shoulders shaking.

'Amy!' Somebody *had* seen her, and her hands came over her face to stem the bubbling laughter as she heard Max's voice behind her. He came swiftly and lightly down to her. 'Amy, are you crying? Oh, Amy, is the pain so bad?'

He sat beside her and moved her hands from her face, his eyes ruefully amused when he saw her laughter and dancing eyes.

'When will I learn?' he breathed. 'Here am I, racing to the rescue, my heart bleeding for you as you sit here crying, and all the time you're simply sitting here enjoying yourself!'

'Not really, Max,' she protested with a grimace. 'I'm on a hunting expedition—there are no pain-killers in my bathroom.'

'Damn, I should have thought of that!' He helped her to her feet and then lifted her. 'They're in the kitchen, as I recall. I'll get you a warm drink.'

'You don't have to look after me, Max,' Amy protested

as he sat her at the kitchen table and drew out a chair for her injured ankle.

'But I want to! Hasn't that thought occurred to you?' Max looked at her steadily as he placed two pain-killers in her hand, and she hastily averted her eyes.

'I don't see why you should.' She was glad when he turned to the fridge and took out some milk, getting a pan to warm it. He must have been reading in his room, she mused. He was still dressed. It was only then that she realised she was undressed, her short nightie and equally short négligé somehow very revealing, although they were not transparent. She drew the ends carefully round her legs, and his eyes flicked over her, noting her action without expression.

'Pretty soon I won't get the chance any more, will I?' he asked softly. 'What with Clive and all, this is probably the last time you'll move in my sphere.'

'I'm not marrying Clive!' Amy insisted, with a little more force than she had intended, then looked quickly away as Max poured the warm milk into a glass and handed it to her.

'But you have your time fully occupied,' he reminded her quietly. 'For all I know, it may be another five years before you come again.'

'You'll be married by then, with children of your own,' she said brightly, her blue eyes escaping from his. She had never intended to get herself into this situation, and Max was having a devastating effect on her.

'Maybe,' he agreed softly. 'Will that be your next excuse for staying away?'

'I haven't been making excuses!' she said sharply, drinking her milk now in one great gulp and pushing the glass away. 'I think I'll hobble back to bed.'

'The kitchen's too hot for you?' he enquired wryly. As she moved abruptly, he pulled her to her feet, but did not lift her; instead, his hands stayed on her shoulders. 'The last time I made hot milk for you, you were a little girl. Now you're all grown up, beautiful as a flower, light as the breeze.'

He folded her against him, and she panicked at once.

'Think of Glenys!' she gasped when his lips brushed over her face.

'I'm too busy thinking of you.'

'It's not fair, Max!'

'Too damned right!' he agreed. 'Nobody should look like you do—you're dangerous. You've even got Seb hot under the collar.'

'Is that why you're doing this?' she asked wildly, turning her face away frantically, her heart beating at an alarming rate with excitement. 'You're punishing me?'

Max laughed, capturing her wildly moving head, his lips inches from hers.

'I haven't actually done anything yet,' he reminded her. 'See if you think it's a punishment.'

He pulled her tightly to him and kissed her with a lingering determination, his lips no longer simply brushing hers as they had done on the sunny hillside, but exploring her mouth with a deep concentration, searching for her reaction, which was instant and instinctive. Amy melted into his arms, her body softly responsive, her eyes still closed as he drew his head away.

'Oh, Amy!' he said in a softly mocking voice. 'You blew it! You needed that.'

She turned away, disregarding her aching ankle and making for the door, but he swept her up into his arms before she had gone more than one step.

'Put me down, you tyrant! You—you sexual monster!'

'Sex is a very powerful emotion, sweet Amy,' he said, laughing into her furious eyes, and she was suddenly subdued.

'I'm very much ashamed,' she confessed, turning her flushed face into his neck, because it was a good place to hide.

'Ashamed? Ashamed of a perfectly natural reaction? I thought you were a modern, self-sufficient person?' Max carried her to the stairs, his voice lowered.

'It's Glenys!'

'But, darling Amy, she's miles away, innocently asleep.' He was laughing at her, and it hurt rather badly. She said nothing else.

In her room, he lowered her to the bed and whisked away her négligée before she could stop him. His face was still amused, and she scrambled into bed, *her* face flushed.

'Don't panic!' he mocked. 'I've already cast you in bronze, nude.'

'Using your imagination!' she said sharply and unwisely. Max nodded slowly, looking down at her.

'Purely for art's sake, I assure you. Nothing to make you worry.'

'I'm not at all worried!' said Amy, with her chin firmly raised, and he ran his fingers along her perfect jawline.

'Not even if I tell you that only the memory of that other figurine, my small and sparky little angel of eleven, prevents me from staying?'

'You have the nerve to imagine I'd let you?'

Max bent quickly, and kissed her hard and fast before releasing her.

'Sex, as I said before, is a very powerful emotion,' he reminded her, his eyes on her dazed face and parted lips.

'It does keep, though.'

He walked out easily, closing the door, and Amy found that both her hands were over her mouth. She had quite got over her crush on Max when she was seventeen, so why was she feeling like this? He was going to marry Glenys. How could he behave like this with her? She had lived a very free and easy life so far, but nobody had ever mistaken her for fair game. It shocked her to think that Max was flirting with her. She couldn't take that. He was too much of a raw male. He was dangerous!

CHAPTER FOUR

AMY had a good night's sleep, with the aid of the pain killers and the warm milk, and by next day the swelling in her ankle was well down, the pain almost gone unless she stood on the foot. At breakfast, Max had treated her as if nothing at all had happened, and she was strangely annoyed about that. Still, if he wanted to forget it, let him; she would see to it that nothing of the sort happened again, and for the life of her she could not feel threatened, not with Max.

She felt trapped, though, unable to move about freely and impatient at this enforced rest that she did not need. Max saw her predicament at lunch time when he came in from the studio, and dealt with it in his usual selfless manner.

'I'll take you for a drive down to the sea,' he offered. 'We'll have a look at the sea and then have tea and cakes at that perfectly horrid little café you used to love.'

'No!' Amy's first reaction was one of self-defence, but his laughing eyes looked into hers and she knew that she wanted to be with him, even if it was a trifle dangerous now.

'Is it still there?' she asked eagerly, then added, 'I can't let you spend your valuable time carting me about, Max!'

'I've done all that I'm doing for today,' he said, and, even though she knew it was solely for her that he was prepared to abandon his work, she was happily excited at the idea of a trip out into the area where she had been so contented in her childhood and teens. Always with Max.

It was still exactly the same. A journey down sunny lanes brought them to the miles of empty sand dunes and the vast expanse of the glittering, grey sea.

'How can people crowd themselves on to beaches in almost every other place, when all the time there's this here, waiting for them?' she asked softly. 'It's so beautiful.'

'You were spoiled by it when you were young,' Max reminded her. 'Most people like to be entertained at the seaside. There's nothing here but nature, the sand-dunes, the sea and the few birdwatchers who wander about from time to time.'

They sat in silence for a while, simply looking out to sea, before Max said, 'Would you like to sit on the sand? The dunes are quite dry and sheltered from the wind.'

Amy's happy smile brought an answering smile to his face, and before long she was snugly deposited in a hollow made by the moving sand, sheltered between high dunes where the tufted grasses grew tall and strong, a view of the sea before her and Max at her side.

'Bliss!' Amy lay back and looked at the blue sky. 'If my friends could see me now!'

'Do you reckon Clive would take to this sort of thing?' Max asked quietly, as he, too, lay looking at the sky.

'Probably not, although I may be doing him an injustice,' she mused. 'He likes the bright lights. He grew up in the city. He likes concerts, the heavy classics, the theatre, things like that.'

'And you don't?'

'Not really. I have this aversion to being forcibly educated. I try to oblige, but I can't say that sitting through gloomy and depressing music and plays with dire messages is quite my style.

She felt Max's eyes on her and kept her own eyes securely on the blue sky, watching the racing clouds. She was telling herself she had no business to be here. Glenys was away, utterly ignorant of the fact that Max was lying here with her, looking at the sky. Her heart was beating faster than it should be, and she had the dreadful feeling that Max knew this perfectly well.

'What's—er—Clive like? Describe him to me,' he ordered, and she hastily cast about in her mind, trying to come up with some Italian film star and not quite managing it.

'He's tall,' she began, improvising glibly. 'He has a sort of—of sheen about him, lovely eyes, large and sort of luminous. He has a moustache, very thick . . .'

'You're describing a walrus—I can hardly wait until you get to the tusks!' Max interrupted, and she turned on her side to face him, doubled up with laughter, holding her stomach, laughing until she ached.

'Oh, Max, you're the funniest person I'll ever know!' she gasped as he turned his head to look at her. 'I really think that you know me better than anyone in the world knows me.'

'So what's he really like?' he asked with a grin, his hand tracing her smiling face. 'No tricks this time.'

'He's tall. He's got brown hair—well, not brown like yours, a sort of light brown. His eyes are hazel. He wears spectacles . . . that's all really, except that he's actually very clever, and of course, I adore him.'

'And you lend him out as a favour,' Max reminded her softly, coming up on one elbow to look down into her face. 'I don't like him! I instinctively know he's not right for you. He probably bores you out of your mind.'

'Frequently!' Amy agreed, turning on to her back and looking up at him. 'He's very attractive, though, in a sensual sort of way.'

'Good God, he's led you from the paths of the righteous! He's got to go!' Max said sardonically, and she looked at him with a daring defiance.

'Heavens, I've had hundreds of boyfriends! Clive isn't the first!'

'Fancy that!' He leaned over her, his strong finger tracing her lips, parting them and moving against the soft moisture inside. It was strangely erotic, terrifyingly so, as it was Max. 'Are you going to set to and describe them all?' he questioned softly, his grey eyes as glittering as the sea as he watched the steady progress of his finger along the softness of her lips.

'You—you asked me about Clive!' Amy protested unsteadily, and his eyes flicked up to meet hers before plunging down again to where his hand traced downwards along the smooth, creamy skin of her neck.

'So I did,' he agreed in a murmur, 'but without too much interest. I really can't take a man seriously who would allow you to simply skip off to come to me.'

'I told you, Aunt Joan blackmailed me,' she said in little more than a whisper. His hands were doing strange things to her, waking feelings she had never felt before, and she panicked when his face lowered towards her, his eyes on her mouth.

'Are you a philanderer, Max?' she got out breathlessly, and saw that secret smile grow along his firm lips, lips that now were so very close.

'Of course! If you hadn't shot off when you were

seventeen, you would have realised it by now.' He came even closer.

'Max!' There was real panic in her voice, but it didn't stop him. His lips brushed hers gently. 'You owe me the feeling of safety. Don't forget that I was a little girl here.'

'Little girls grow up, thank God,' he said in a murmur. 'You're secure, Blue Eyes! Kissing me isn't going to change your life dramatically, especially with all your experience of men.'

It would, though, and she knew it, but it was impossible to get away, even if she had been really trying. Max's lips closed over hers and she gave up the idea of any struggle because it was like stepping into another world, a world where only she and Max could dwell. So many things happened to her; a great soaring feeling of joy, a great shaft of pain that hit her stomach and weakened her legs and a terrible, terrible sweetness that she knew she would never feel again, whoever kissed her. She had been waiting for this from the moment she had seen him again, expecting it with a breathless excitement.

For a second, Max raised his head and looked down into her dazed eyes, his hand gentle on her face, and then, very carefully, he moved her into his arms, lying across her, his powerful chest crushing her tender, aching breasts.

'Max!' She managed his name just once and then his lips captured hers again, moving over hers with a searching intensity that robbed her mind of all power to think, as his hand slowly and gently moved over her shoulder, moulding the slender bones, stroking across her breast to rest there possessively.

'Oh, please!' She tore her mouth away, her hand plucking frantically at his, her movements losing their determination when he rubbed this thumb softly back and forth across the tight bud of her nipple.

'Sweet Amy, I'm not hurting you. Inside you're all eagerness and warmth. You're waiting for me. I know you, Amy! I know you as I know myself.'

'You'll hurt me,' she whispered, her body trembling uncontrollably.

'Never!' he murmured against her lips, and when he kissed her again, her hand stayed over his, silently acknowledging his right to touch her.

Within seconds there was no other world but the one that held her to Max. The tangy smell of his skin was in her nostrils, a smell she had grown up with and would have recognised anywhere. There was nothing about him to frighten her, only an aching sweetness, a gentle and tender tugging at her heart, mind and body. Slowly and inexorably, he was drawing her as close to his soul as he already held her close to his body, and her own reaction was one of sheer wonder.

Her teenage dreams of Max had never been like this. In her slightly erotic dreams at seventeen, he had been powerful and overbearing, demanding her love. Now, he demanded nothing. His power was there for her to feel, but it was tightly controlled, leashed in like the force of a storm that threatened to break but waited still for the first roll of thunder. Instead he called to her, silently and gently, luring her into a whirlpool of feeling that would soon overwhelm her.

Her slender arms were tightly around his neck, her body pressed close to his and her head thrown back in welcoming submission as his lips trailed across the creamy skin of her face, when, deep in her subconscious mind, she heard a great deal of sound. Max heard it too and stiffened, his head lifting from her as he listened. They might have been in the middle of a crowd. Certainly there were people close by, plenty of people, although there was not one to be seen.

With one lithe movement Max sat up and looked over the dunes, and Amy saw the tension leave his shoulders as he began to laugh quietly.

'I'll be damned! Look here!' He took her hand and drew her, unresisting, to a sitting position, so that she too could look over the dunes at the wide stretch of beach, the deserted beach that was now deserted no more. There must have been thirty people, possibly more. They were geared for walking, haversacks on their backs, stout boots on their feet, and they approached in that disciplined but haphazard manner that spoke of an organised party of ramblers.

'Saved by vast numbers!' said Amy with a shaky attempt at humour, and Max turned clear grey eyes on her, eyes that neither reproached nor apologised. Instead, his gaze roamed over her flushed and bewildered face and, as the party at last moved out of sight, he stood smoothly and pulled her to her feet, swinging her straight up into his arms.

If he would say something, anything! Amy bit into her lip and tried to control the rapid beating of her heart. If they hadn't come, if she had simply let Max . . . She would never be able to look at him again, because he knew what she knew perfectly well herself—that she had wanted him badly, feelings that she had never felt before. Things would never be the same.

'I'd like to go back now, please,' she said in a low voice,

avoiding his eyes when they were once again in the car.

'First the café. You were promised tea and cakes, and I never break my word.'

'I—I can't! Not now!' She twisted her hands together and turned her face away, but his strong hand turned it back to him, tilting it and forcing her to meet his eyes.

'Was making love with me so traumatic that you can't even face tea and cakes?' he enquired softly, his eyes roaming over her face.

'We didn't! We didn't make love!' she protested, her cheeks glowing, but his slow smile silenced her.

'But we wanted to. Both of us wanted that. The only difference between us is that I had every intention of stopping.'

There was no answer that she could make, and as Max still held her face she had no defence when he leaned across and kissed her soundly on the lips before releasing her.

'Now for the dreadful café!' he announced, and she could see it meant nothing to him at all. It had altered her life, she thought. She gave a small, tragic sigh, turning away, and when she glanced at him, he was watching the road with all the appearance of a man at peace, perfectly calm, driving along as if they had just left the house and none of it had ever happened. He had gone a long way towards seducing her, she reasoned wildly, and here he was, simply contented!

'I hate you!' she said in a strangled voice, her hands tightly clenched. To her great shame and utter fury, Max threw back his handsome head and roared with laughter.

'I know! I can feel it radiating from you like the fire from a well stoked furnace.'

'Got it in one!' she snapped. 'The trust of a lifetime is over. From now on, I'm your enemy!'

'Only until I hold you again,' he said softly, 'and you know I'm going to do that.'

It silenced her, and he made her take tea and cakes too, but by the time they reached Belmore House, Amy's shame had subsided and with it her temper. It was impossible to sustain the feeling of shame when he talked to her across the table at the café and treated her as if nothing had happened at all. If that was the way he wanted it, then it was all right by her, but, when he lifted her from the car at the house and she automatically put her arm around his neck, he looked down into her face and tightened her to him, his eyes bright with promise, and all her shame re-surfaced as the piercing feelings shot through her again. There was Glenys to consider, and it mattered to her, even if, as it seemed, Max was prepared to ignore the fact that he was almost engaged.

Just before dinner, right out of the blue, Glenys appeared, clearly taking Max by surprise. If her absence last night had provoked Max to temper with Sebastian, then it was obvious that she too was distressed when Max was out of her sight—as well she might be, Amy thought darkly, looking at them as they spoke softly to each other at dinner. Apparently her cousin was remarkably recovered and Glenys had driven here straight from Durham. Fortunate that she had not arrived in the early afternoon and come to seek them out, Amy thought, her cheeks glowing as she relived the moments when she had clung to Max at the beach.

If Max had recovered his temper, it was clear that

Sebastian had not, and Amy found herself once again being overwhelmed by his attention. She had never known him talk so much or drink so much, and after a while it became very necessary to keep him by her in order to protect him both from Max's growing annoyance at his antics and from his own likelihood of making a perfect fool of himself.

The climax to the dramatic day came when Sebastian loudly insisted on helping her to her bedroom. Amy agreed gladly, for two reasons. One, she had no intention of being in Max's arms, and two, there was every chance that, once upstairs, Sebastian would stay there. As it turned out, her gallant attempt to protect him brought out the worst in everyone.

Now very much the worse for drink, Sebastian entered the giddy stage, laughing and overly bright, not too steady on his feet, and Amy declined his offer to carry her, feeling uneasy enough as it was with her arm around him as he half lifted and half dragged her up the stairs, her hopping merely helping to unbalance him.

She humoured him, laughing gaily at his antics, her eyes bright with false amusement when she glanced back and saw both Max and a pale-faced Glenys watching from the hall.

Max was furious, but it was Glenys's face that caught and held Amy's gaze. She was looking up at Max with her heart in her eyes, tragically aware that he had wanted to carry Amy himself. It could not have been more clear.

'That's just about far enough!' Max bounded up the stairs and whisked Amy into his arms, turning furious eyes on Sebastian. 'If you've quite finished mauling Amy, pehaps you could give some consideration to having an early night!' he snapped.

'I was helping Amy! I wasn't in any way—mauling!' Sebastian stated with a noble attempt at dignity. 'I'm quite capable of getting Amy up to her room!'

'Or down to the bottom of the stairs on her head!' Max retorted disgustedly. 'Face it, Seb, you've had too much wine for the first time in your life. For God's sake, get to bed!'

He took the rest of the flight two at a time and deposited Amy on her bed, none too gently.

'Don't you ever try waving Seb under my nose like that again!' he ground out violently. 'He can't take flirtatious behaviour, and Glenys is shocked out of her mind!'

'I was not flirting with Sebastian! I was merely trying to protect him from himself and from your temper!' Amy lay sprawled across the bed where he had almost thrown her, her brilliantly blue eyes sparkling with rage, her white dress almost up over her knees.

'Normally I would have been prepared to believe that,' he said with a menacing quiet, 'but as you've declared war on me, I know you well enough to know you'll take any chance that comes, even if it's Sebastian!'

'That's a perfectly rotten thing to say!' Amy shouted, mindless of the power of her voice. 'You were just feeling guilty about this afternoon, and the guilty credit everyone else with their crimes. Sebastian is still a gentleman! The mauling was in your mind only!'

'Lower your voice and re-think your attitude,' advised Max softly, his furious grey eyes flaring over her body, 'or I might just take Glenys home and then come back to you. I think it wouldn't take too long to show you the difference between mauling and the way I treated you this afternoon!'

He strode out of the room, slamming the door, and Amy lay as he had left her, her eyes bright with a mixture of temper and tears. This was not her beloved Max! It just showed how things fell apart when the ugly face of sex reared its head. The thought of that brought other thoughts that she had no intention of thinking, and she turned a tight face to the door when a soft knock announced the arrival of Bernice.

'I can't believe it!' Bernice said dramatically. 'I actually saw Max and Sebastian almost fighting over you, while poor Glenys stood in the hall so tragically! What's happening?'

'It was all a stupid misunderstanding,' Amy said quickly, hoping the excuse would silence Bernice.

'God, I hope so! I've never seen Max angry with you before, ever. Let's hope things improve tomorrow!'

'They will,' Amy said determinedly, turning her hot and angry face into the pillow and thumping it to release some of the strain on her mind and body. 'Tomorrow I'm going home!'

In the morning, though, she changed her mind, and Sebastian was the reason for that. He tapped on her door when he was ready for work and came in with an embarrassed smile when she called to him.

'Sebastian—is something wrong?' Amy sat up in bed and looked at him worriedly. He looked so dreadful.

'Everything, I should think. I made a complete fool of myself last night.' This morning, he was gloomy and pale. The drink had left him feeling under the weather, and he was very much ashamed, that much was clear. Amy's heart went out to him.

'Come and sit by your Auntie Amy!' she said firmly, patting the bed, and he smiled a little uneasily, coming to sit beside her on the bed.

'Did I really maul you, Amy?' he asked anxiously as he sat down.

'Most certainly not! I was furious with Max!'

'I heard you shouting,' he confessed. 'I'm sorry if I've caused trouble between you. I mean, Max has always spoiled you. I've never heard him angry with you before, and I know it was my fault.'

'Max is not without faults,' Amy said firmly, 'and so far, I've found no fault at all with you. All you did was get a little giddy. Once in a while it's good for you.'

'Anyway,' said Sebastian truculently, 'I didn't make you have a sprained ankle. That was Max's fault!'

'Absolutely true!' Amy agreed treacherously. 'Set your mind at rest: Max is no angel!'

'Glenys thinks so. I can't see why I shouldn't enjoy your company when Max is occupied with Glenys full-time. It's definitely a dog-in-the-manger attitude.'

Something that should have been glaringly obvious dawned on Amy.

'You—er—you're rather fond of Glenys, aren't you?' she asked quietly. Sebastian's red face told her all she really wanted to know, but he felt close enough to her, apparently, to confess.

'Yes, I am. I've been fond of her for ages. Then Max appeared on the scene. Not that I'd done anything about it, Amy. I—I find it rather difficult. I made a bit of a fool of myself last night, but it doesn't really matter, Glenys never notices me. Just so long as you're not annoyed with me . . .'

'I'm not, Seb. I understand.' And how she understood! He smiled more brightly and leaned forward to kiss her cheek.

'Oh, thanks, Amy! I feel I can face the day now. I've been feeling awful about last night.'

'Nonsense!' Amy said heartily. 'You're a very wonderful person, I quite enjoyed the excitement.' She returned the kiss, her lips brushing his cheek gently—then her eyes opened in horror as she looked up to see Max standing in the open doorway.

She had no idea why she should feel so guilty. The door was open, Sebastian had wanted to talk to her, and in any case, he was like a brother. Even so, her cheeks flushed hotly, and Max looked quite disgusted.

'Don't you think you should have closed the door, Sebastian?' he asked coldly, and Sebastian turned round, getting up quickly, Max's unexpected arrival and aggressive attitude bringing back all his worries and nervous tension. It infuriated Amy and her blue eyes began to flash sparks.

'The door is mine!' she snapped with an aggression of her own. 'Sebastian wanted a word with me before he went off to work, though why either of us should feel like explaining to you is quite beyond me!'

Sebastian, seeing the storm brewing, had the good sense to leave with a muttered goodbye. He knew when he was outclassed, and he could see the light of battle in both their eyes.

'Is it also beyond you to have just one man at a time?' asked Max with a deadly quiet, as soon as Sebastian was out of hearing range. 'I would have thought Douglas Heaton would have been enough to keep you going, bearing in mind that there's always Clive hanging about in the background in a discreet sort of way. Sebastian can't take this kind of thing. Leave him alone!'

'Remember what I told you last night about the guilty being quick to credit others with their own crimes?' Amy snapped, her face flushed with anger. 'You forgot to add yourself to the long list of my indiscretions! Furthermore,' she added, before he could express the fury that was on his face, 'I was merely assuring Sebastian that I wasn't angry or horrified that he had a little too much to drink last night. I wasn't looking for excitement!'

'And don't ever!' grated Max, 'because if you ever again give me cause to be suspicious that you're trying to trap Sebastian, I'll give you more excitement than you can handle!'

'Don't bank on it!' Amy raged, quite beside herself, climbing out of bed the better to face him. 'After yesterday, I'll see you coming—a long way off!'

'And run straight towards me!' he sneered, his eyes flaring over her in her short blue nightie. 'Lucky for you that you weren't giving Seb this kind of treat when I came to the door, or the door would be firmly locked by now and you'd be learning a few new lessons!'

'Out! Get out! Get out!' Wild with rage and embarrassment, Amy snatched up a pillow and threw it at him, enraged even further to see him field it neatly and toss it back with easy grace to its exact position on the bed. He went, though, his eyes threatening and as icily grey as the cold sea.

Amy tried her foot. In her annoyance she had simply

stood up, ignoring any pain, quite forgetting it, in fact, but she felt it as she put her weight on the foot now. Even so, she was much better, and she would not countenance being carried about any more—not, she reminded herself, that Max would be wanting to. He would probably like the chance to drop her from the top of the stairs and see if she bounced!

He had disappeared when she went down, and she begged a stick from her aunt Dorothy, pleased to find she could get about quite well with that, fairly sure she would be completely better by the next day. When Bernice suggested that they drive into the town to do a little shopping and get the children an ice-cream, Amy readily agreed, praying that Max would stay in his studio, bashing hell out of some inoffensive lump of rock. Apparently he was doing just that, according to Bernice.

'More trouble?' enquired Bernice as they sat with coffee in the town and watched the children eating peach Melbas with astonishing speed.

'Only a re-run of last night's,' Amy said wearily. 'I don't know Max any more. I used to think the sun shone from him. Now I don't even know him. I have no idea why he's so hostile to me.'

'Mmm,' Bernice mused darkly, 'I could venture a guess, but don't let it drive you away. You're mine too, and Aunt Dorothy's and Simon's and Cheryl's and . . .'

'Stop!' laughed Amy. 'You make me feel as if I'm to be spread thinly on the ground!'

'So long as you realise how valuable you are!' Bernice insisted.

It made Amy feel much better, except that she would have to face Max at dinner.

As it turned out, she was spared that too, because as they returned to Belmore House, Douglas rang and asked if she would like to go out to dinner with him. She was never so happy to agree to anything in her whole life, and he was quite taken aback by her rather desperate acceptance.

During the day, her foot had improved even more, and although she still needed the stick, she managed quite well. Douglas made a great deal of fuss over her, something that normally she would have found quite tiresome, but after her battle with Max she felt somewhat shaken and mournful, and it was good to be fussed over like an invalid.

She enjoyed the evening too, even if her mind did keep wandering treacherously back to Max and the way his arms had held her on the soft sand. She was glad she would not have to face him when she got back, because it was clear that Douglas would be keeping her out as late as he could, and she made no move to bring the evening to an end. It suited her to be late in; with any luck, Max would be in bed.

The house was in darkness, except for the light in the hall, but she had begged a key from her aunt and she let herself in quietly.

'Can you manage?' Douglas stood in the doorway as Amy walked carefully in with her stick.

'Yes, thank you.' They were both whispering, and the humour of it struck them both at the same time, making them splutter with laughter as Amy said goodnight and closed the door.

She began her journey to the stairs, leaving her stick in the hall, a little overwhelmed when she saw the height she would have to climb, a great sigh escaping from her as she stood for a moment to contemplate this mountain.

Max appeared at the top of the stairs, watching her, and she had no idea how long he had been there. She ducked her head and began to climb, feeling utterly dispirited and not a little tearful. She couldn't think Max would ever speak to her again. The whole thing was so awful! She had gone out tonight simply to escape from him, to escape from Max!

He came down the stairs lightly and quickly, taking them two at a time, and before she could protest she was lifted into his arms and he was carrying her up the stairs, but he never spoke. This was a service only, a kindness no doubt brought on because he had been the one who had insisted that she visit his house. Not that he had not always been kind to her.

He simply put her down at her door and walked off to his room, leaving her with tears in her eyes for the first time in years. Amy could hardly remember when she had last cried. Her temper had always surfaced long before her tears, but she cried then, as soon as she was safely in her room.

CHAPTER FIVE

THE NEXT DAY, the whole family had planned to go to Durham Cathedral, where there was a service for children, and Amy had intended to go too, but she begged to be excused. This morning her foot felt quite better, but as they were certain to be walking a great deal she thought it wise to stay behind. Of course, there were protests, especially from the children, but she finally convinced them that it would only set her back several days to go. She had had sprains before, she told them, and she really knew what she was talking about. It was all quite true, and they finally left, leaving her in the house alone.

The housekeeper was going too, and Amy would not hear of her staying behind. She wanted some time to herself. This whole affair with Max had really upset her and she intended to leave in the morning, but it was a painful decision.

Of course Max wasn't going; he was out even before Amy got up, going to chase some equipment that had failed to arrive, and her aunt Dorothy warned her that they would not be back before teatime, Amy assuring her with a wide smile that she was not afraid of being alone. In fact, if Max had been staying she would certainly have gone with them—but she kept this snippet of information to herself.

As it turned out, she was too afraid to think. She was beginning to hide from her feelings for Max; they were too deep, too intense. She wanted no such feelings. Max was beyond her reach, she told herself firmly, recoiling then from that thought, as it admitted that she wanted to reach him. She refused to think about it any more and spent the greater part of the day reading, making her own lunch and enjoying doing it.

It was almost six o'clock when the sky suddenly turned dark and the storm that had been forecast on the earlier news began to make itself felt around the old house. It began with the wind, so strong that it rocked the great old trees in the park. Then the rain began, slowly at first, but the drops sizeable, a foretaste of the downpour to come.

Amy was watching the gathering of the storm from the drawing-room window when she saw Smithers trapped in the tree close to the house. For a cat who had so far managed to escape detection even though she had looked for him, he was now making his presence known. She could not hear his cries above the noise of the wind, but his face was very clear, his mouth wide open as he yelled for help.

Amy dashed out, her foot and its troubles forgotten, just getting to the tree as the deluge broke. Within seconds she was soaked, her white jeans and her thin sweater darkened with water, but she kept on resolutely, climbing to the first bough with no difficulty, even though it was now very slippery with the rain.

She was hauled furiously down, her legs flying, her heart leaping with shock to see Max angrily pulling her into his arms.

'Smithers!' she protested, but she was glad not to be able to hear what he said; she could tell from his face that it was not a word for her ears.

She found herself being taken none too kindly to the kitchen, noticing in a rather vague manner that they were leaving a trail of water that marked their progress.

'I —I didn't know you were here!' she offered, making it sound like an excuse.

'And I didn't know *you* were here!' Max snapped angrily, 'otherwise I would have taken precautions to protect myself from being soaked. I came in and went straight to the studio at least two hours ago. Why didn't you go with the others?' he asked aggressively, opening the kitchen door and forcing her inside.

'M-my foot.' He was quite frightening her, and her temper was nowhere in sight.

'Look at you, you're soaked to the skin!' For a moment Amy felt the flicker of fear as his anger washed over her, the lightning of his silvery eyes striking her like a physical force.

'Smithers,' she began in a shaken way. 'He—he was trapped . . . he still is.'

She had to look away, his anger was unbearable, and he let her go so suddenly that she staggered. He reached for a warm towel that was by the big Aga and turned back to her.

'Now you're wet and miserable, to say nothing of the fact that you put yourself in danger climbing that tree in this weather! Don't you know, for God's sake, that cats do that and then climb down and walk off when nobody pays them any attention?'

'He—he's old!' she reminded him, getting a snort of anger for her pains.

'Old enough to recognise a fool when he sees one. He'll be grinning all over his feline face now!' Max looked at her with intense annoyance. 'Anyway, your clothes are wet through. Go and get a hot shower!'

She was just letting him growl at her, but she couldn't

seem to answer back right now.

'You're wet too, Max,' she ventured huskily, her eyes on the broad shoulders and the fine woollen sweater that was dark with water.

'Yes—thanks to you and that damned cat!' He pulled the wet sweater impatiently over his head, draping it over the kitchen chair, giving his hair a cursory rub with the warm towel. 'Go and get that shower!'

'All right. I—I'm sorry, Max.' Amy turned away quickly before he could see she had tears in her eyes. What had happened to her and to Max, that this was the way he behaved towards her? Was her crime so very great?

'Oh, come here!' He reached out and spun her roughly towards him, covering her wet hair in the thickness and warmth of the towel as he began, with more vigour than gentleness, to dry the shining black hair.

'You're hurting me!' He had never given her the chance to look up, and all she could think of was the harshness of his touch, the cruel way he rubbed her head with the towel.

'Roll with the punches, then!' The words were a deep growl as she struggled to keep her footing under the onslaught of his powerful hands.

'Please, Max!' In desperation Amy moved closer, her forehead resting against the hard brown nakedness of his chest, and for a second he stiffened, his hands stilled, and then he continued to rub her hair with more care as his anger seemed to lessen.

'You scared me, you little idiot!' His voice was curiously thick, and her hands sought his waist to steady herself, but she moved them quickly to his belt as she felt him flinch at her touch.

'I'm sorry, I didn't mean to,' she said in a muffled voice.

'To what?'

'To scare you. Is—is that why you're so angry?'

'Why else?' There was mockery in his voice now, and suddenly she couldn't bear it. She wanted him back. She wanted Max as he had always been—tender, caring for her. Her thick lashes flickered open, and all she could see was the brown power of his chest, the strong muscles. The warm, masculine smell of him was in her nostrils, the scent and feel of him filling her with a wild longing she had never quite known before, even when he had kissed her on the beach. With a little moan of desperation, she pressed her soft lips to the smooth strength of his chest.

'Amy!' A shudder seemed to rock his whole body and he jerked her head up, gripping it fiercely, staring into her blue, bemused eyes. 'Why did you do that? Are you crazy, for God's sake?'

He was furious, and Amy closed her eyes to escape the sparkling anger that threatened to devastate her. Of course he was furious—he thought she was playing the games he suspected her of. And there was Glenys! Why had she done it? She felt her timid caress was a monstrous liberty, even though he had caressed her on the beach, and tears escaped from her tightly shut eyes.

It was no use being cowardly, though. She looked up at him, her blue eyes enormous in her pale face.

'Why did you do that?' Max was not angry any more, and the towel fell to the floor as he gently cupped her face, his eyes on the softness of her trembling lips.

'I—I wanted to . . . it—it just happened.' It was no excuse and she knew it. She was whispering, a pleading in her eyes.

'Why aren't you fighting me?' he asked softly. 'Where's the little spitfire who gives me the sharp edge of her tongue, who throws pillows at me?'

Amy couldn't answer, she just went on looking at him, and he drew her closer.

'Amy!' Her name was a deep whisper on his lips as his mouth sought hers. Everything in her rose to meet him, and his mouth became urgent as he felt her instant response.

His lips parted hers with a hungry need that was unlike anything she had ever dreamed of, and suddenly she wanted to give him everything, recognising the love she felt; it had started when she was seventeen, and although she had hidden it carefully it had never gone.

'Oh, God, this is madness!' The knowledge that Max's hoarse whisper proclaimed did not stop him. His lips trailed kisses of fire across her cheeks and, as his hands slid to her narrow hips to urge her even closer, she wound her arms around his neck, the hard pressure of his thighs arousing her still further.

'Amy, you're so beautiful, like a dream that drives a man mad,' he whispered thickly against her skin, and then his mouth was devouring her again as his hands slid beneath her wet sweater to caress the warmth of her skin. She heard herself moaning softly as his fingers moved sensuously over her, sliding around her ribcage to lift and search eagerly for the pointed swell of her breasts.

She was aglow with the wonder of it, her rediscovered love, her legs weak, her senses clamouring for more as his heart pounded over hers.

Then suddenly she was free, her arms snatched from around his neck, held firmly to her sides by his iron grip. For a second he stared at her, his face white except for the deep flush along his high cheekbones, his breathing ragged in his throat.

'Max?' She was too dazed to recognise his rejection as she stared at him wildly, her brilliant blue eyes wide open, the surrender in them all too plain for him to see.

'I must be out of my mind!' With a muttered oath, he grabbed his sweater and walked out of the room, leaving her alone and trembling, and within minutes she heard the sound of the cars returning as everyone else came home. Max had lost his head, but he had remembered in time that he was getting married to Glenys. Amy fled to her room to the shower, to privacy, and for the first time in her life, to a deluge of tears.

In the morning it turned out that Max was away. He had left the house early, and his absence gave Amy the chance she needed. It wasn't difficult to convince either of her aunts that she had to return to London. In just over a week's time she was due to take a party of the older children to Paris for five days, and a few muttered worries about organisation settled their minds about her departure.

She felt very guilty. Lying was not easy for her, it sat heavily on her conscience for, in fact, the organisation had already been done by the headmaster, who was to accompany the party, and Amy was only one of the three members of staff going. But she had to get away from Max!

Her ankle felt better, and she set off for the station with Sebastian as he left for work. But even as she sat in the train, looking out of the window as it pulled from the station, she realised she was not really waving goodbye to Sebastian. Her eyes were looking over his head, searching for Max, wondering where he was, how long he would be, a forlorn hope in her that he would tear into the station and demand that she stay. But he did not.

He was going to marry Glenys. Amy tried to drill the thought into her mind, to shut Max out of it. Unfortunately, she could still feel his arms around her, his lips searching hers and, now that her temper could help her no more, the magic of yesterday flooded her heart and mind, washed over her body and left her weak.

She wanted Max! She wanted to be with him. He had awakened feelings that had been there for years and now she could not simply shut them out. She was facing months of misery and the realisation that she would never again be able to visit Belmore House. To imagine Max married to Glenys was too painful to think about. To be invited to the wedding would be a nightmare, a similar sort of nightmare to the one that Sebastian would face. She would once again abandon her friends in Northumberland and concentrate on her life in London.

She threw herself into a frenzy of housework when she arrived home, wilfully ignoring her weak ankle and doing jobs that she and Aunt Joan had been threatening to do for months, so that by the next day her ankle was swollen again and she had to rest it.

Clive rang in the afternoon and, finding her at home, he called in to see her, eagerly describing the concert and Kitty's reaction to it, which apparently had been most pleasing. He too was going on the trip to Paris, and on his second visit he came armed with pamphlets that he had collected. Amy made a note to get her ankle back into shape. It was clear that nothing would be neglected in their week in France.

Her enthusiasm for school, for the trip, for sport and for almost anything else had left her, and she knew why. She had suspected as she lay in Max's arms that it was the end of her days of carefree enjoyment, and she had not been mistaken. He was in her mind all the time, refusing to be supplanted by any activity, any other thought. By the beginning of the week her ankle was better and she started doing a few simple exercises to strengthen it, but everything she did was half-hearted.

She was greatly pleased, therefore, when, on Monday night, Robert Stokes knocked on the door, suitcase in hand, and she didn't need to ask what he wanted. Many of the people she had known at college used this house as a hotel for the night. It had begun when she had been still at college, and had continued ever since. From time to time, the spare room was occupied for one night only by her friends who were passing through London on their way north or south. Few of them could afford hotels even now, and her aunt delighted in putting them up for the night, giving them supper and breakfast and then turning out the room, ready for the next arrival.

Amy sat up until late, mulling over old times with Robert, talking about their present jobs, and it was almost nine before she surfaced the following morning, and Robert was still fast asleep. She pulled on her jeans and T-shirt and hastily washed, racing downstairs to get his breakfast as she called to him. He wanted to get the ten-thirty train, and she knew he would have to move fast if he was to make it in time.

Even before she had made a pot of tea the doorbell rang, and she hurried to answer it, her black hair a little unruly, her cheeks still flushed from sleep. Shock waves of feeling hit her when she opened the door and found Max waiting impatiently on the step.

'Max!' Amy just stared at him, and he reached forward and lifted her out of his way.

'Full marks for keen observation!' he praised sardonically, stepping into the hall.

'What—what are you doing here?' Even the sight of him had her hands trembling, and she hastily pushed them into the back pockets of her jeans.

'You know why I'm here, though if you want a long and involved explanation I'm sure I can come up with something.' His eyes ran over her flushed face, her untidy hair, then rested on the tightness of her breasts beneath the T-shirt. Amy quickly folded her arms, avoiding his raised eyebrows by indicating the sitting-room door.

'If you'd care to sit down?'

'How very civilised!' Any further comment he would have made died in his throat as Robert appeared at the top of the stairs, suitcase in hand, struggling to get into his jacket. He too looked a little wild, Amy thought guiltily, and her eyes slid to Max's face.

She had never seen Max look quite like that before, and it frightened her. His face was like stone, his eyes blazing, a clear and silvery grey. The muscles in his jaw tightened and bunched together, and the fury in his face, as Robert stopped half-way down the stairs and looked at him in surprise, was quite apparent.

'Oh, hi! Robert Stokes.' He held out his hand, but the sight of Max's face was enough for him to withdraw it rapidly. Max had never looked so big! Amy for once had no easy or flippant remark to make, and it was left to Robert to fill the menacing silence.

'I've got to dash. Thanks for a warm night, love. I'll see you soon.'

'But you—you haven't had your breakfast. You haven't even had a drink!'

'Not to worry, I'll get something at the station. 'Bye,

Amy!' He gave her a quick peck on the cheek and walked out through the open front door, very obviously feeling this was an escape situation, every man for himself. Amy slowly closed the door and turned to face Max. She felt guilty when there was no cause for it, angry at his attitude and shaken by his arrival.

'Well, would you like to sit down, then?' she said a trifle breathlessly, but he ignored her.

'Who was that?' He looked very dangerous, but even so, she tried her old tactics.

'Robert Stokes, as he said. If you'd shaken hands and had a kind word for him, he would have undoubtedly told you more.'

'What more is there to tell?' Max ground out savagely. 'He already mentioned the warm night that you've spent together!'

Amy lashed out at him, furious that Max should think this of her, but he caught her hand none too gently and merely used it to draw her close to his taut and savage body.

'We did not spend the night together!' she snapped, her blue eyes spitting sparks. 'There are always people like that here. Aunt Joan lets them stay the night on their way through London!'

'Your aunt Joan isn't here!' he grated. 'Does she know you have men in the house when she's away?'

'I do *not* have men in the house! Robert is an old friend, and it's quite normal for friends to stay.'

'So long as they stay in their own beds! This one had a warm night—and so did you, by the look of you!'

'Get out!' Amy pulled free and pointed furiously at the door. 'Get out of here, Max, and don't bother to come back, ever! I can't think why you're here in the first place, because I don't need you to tell me how to run my life!'

'I came here to take you back, because I want you back!' he said tightly. 'I didn't expect to find you with another man.'

'Oh, God, I wasn't with another man!' Amy ran her fingers wildly through her crisp black hair. 'Even if I was, though, it has nothing whatever to do with you! Now, please go, Max!'

For a moment he stared at her with angry eyes, then he pulled her roughly to him, lashing his arms around her and tilting her face to his, his hands twisting into her hair, painfully tight.

'All right! First, though, I'll kiss you goodbye!'

It was an angry kiss, fierce and heated, burning her lips and leaving her shaken and trembling. Then he was gone. He simply released her and walked out, slamming the door behind him with a great deal of violence, and Amy leaned against the hall table, her face in her hands, her eyes filled with tears.

She seemed to stand there for ages, her thoughts in turmoil. Max had come for her. He had been furiously jealous to find Robert here. There was no mistaking his emotion—it was pure male aggression, open and violent jealousy. Amy was too upset, too shocked to think what it all meant, and her own feelings swung from one thing to another. She had wanted him to come to the station and demand that she stay; instead, he had waited and then come all the way down here.

What did he feel for her? She was not even quite sure if she dared think about it. It was easy enough to mistake desire for love; she had done so herself before and then grown out of it. Only the strange feeling of possession that she had felt in his new house had unsettled her, until he had held her close and kissed her. Did Max feel it, too? Did he realise what there was between them now?

A sound jolted her into life and her head lifted from her hands, her face flushing more deeply as she saw Max standing there in the open doorway.

'How did you get back in?' She had meant to be aggressive herself, but it somehow came out all wrong.

'I lifted the latch as I left, knowing your frame of mind and your odd character. I knew I hadn't the slightest chance of getting back in except under my own steam.'

'I asked you to leave!' Amy straightened and looked squarely at him, valiantly ignoring the tears that still swam in her eyes.

'I know.' Max's grey eyes were intent on her small heart-shaped face, a smile growing in the silvery-grey depths. 'Coming?'

Amy just stared at him, unable to look away, all the fight and tension draining from her.

'I—I had to get away . . . Don't you see, Max?'

'I do see. But I never asked why you left, I only asked if you were coming back.' He stepped closer and stood looking down at her, and the few tears overflowed on to her cheeks as she nodded, partly defeatedly, partly in glorious acceptance of his almost mystical right to own her.

He pulled her against him, cradling her head to his chest, his hand caressing her hair.

'Pack your things,' he ordered softly. 'I'll get you some breakfast on the way. I want you out of here and out of harm's way as quickly as possible.'

'I'm not in any . . .' She lifted her head, tense again and ready to fight as usual, but he put one strong finger across her lips, silencing her.

'Not now. Later, when you're fed and trapped in my car.'

'Did you come down especially for me?' asked Amy wonderingly as they drove north. To her chagrin, Max laughed softly and shook his head.

'I had to come down this week—there's an exhibition that demanded a conference. I got here the night before last.'

And never even phoned me, Amy thought miserably. Why had she come? Why was she sitting here like a fool beside him, bowing to his wishes? He had come to see her on a whim, and if she had not been in he would have gone back to Northumberland and thought nothing more about it. He had probably put the thought of that afternoon on the beach, and the wild passion between them when they were alone in the house, right out of his mind. One day she would learn to obey her instincts and not follow her heart.

Her reception at Belmore House lifted her spirits, though. Bernice was there until the end of the week and her husband Jack had at last arrived. The children greeted her with squeals of delight, wanting to know if her ankle was better, very obviously planning a display of gymnastics for their father's benefit, but Amy got out of that easily.

The next few days took on a pattern that seemed to be unvaried. With Bernice and her husband, excited children in tow, Amy roamed the county she loved so well, picnicking on the hills, playing with the children on the beach, enduring Glenys at dinner time and being especially careful in her dealings with Sebastian. She wanted no more trouble in that direction. As to Max, he worked, all day and every day, only appearing before dinner in time to bring Glenys to the house with unfailing and boring regularity, and Amy felt the deep pangs of jealousy herself. Having brought her here he was no longer interested in what she did at all. Glenys was the set pattern in his life.

On one of their expeditions into the village with the children, Amy and Bernice ran into Douglas Heaton and he invited Amy to accompany him on his rounds before she left for London again. She was delighted to accept; it would be something to take her mind off Max. All she was doing now was watching for him to leave the studio and come into the house. She invited Douglas to dinner too, quite wilfully. She needed to build a defence against seeing Max constantly with Glenys. She needed him to know that there was more to her life than him.

It did not have the desired effect. Max was merely amused and appeared to think it a great idea that Amy should spend the next day going round the farms with Douglas. She would normally have enjoyed it, but she did not, and she returned home quite dispirited, knowing she had been a poor companion.

Max looked at her long and hard, and then simply smiled. He was so sure of her! How had she got into this situation? She didn't really need to ask herself that. Max had got her into this situation.

It was only on the last day that Max deigned to notice her presence. He came in early from his studio and greeted Sebastian with a great deal of good humour.

'Can I beg a favour, Seb?' he asked with a wry grin.

'It depends what it is,' said Sebastian with an answering smile, and Amy could see that they did not need her to straighten things out between them; they were as close as they had ever been. As usual, the only loser was herself.

'I wondered if you'd go and collect Glenys for dinner tonight? I did say I'd be there, and she's expecting to come, but I've got something else to do. If you'd bring her here and entertain her at dinner, then take her back later, I'd be really grateful.'

Amy was almost open-mouthed at this piece of cheek. She expected Sebastian to be annoyed and shocked, but he was nothing of the sort.

'Oh, sure, I'd be glad to. I do know her from work, after all.'

'Well, she's been coming here long enough for you to know her, anyway,' Max pointed out. 'Thanks, Seb. It's Amy's last night here and I want to take her out to dinner.'

Now Amy *was* open-mouthed.

'But Glenys will . . .'

'She'll understand perfectly well,' Max said firmly. 'She likes coming here and she knows Seb. For God's sake, she works with him, she likes him!'

'But . . . but this is different, surely you can see that?'

'Do her good to be forced into talking to other people,' said Max with clinical certainty, and to her annoyance, Sebastian nodded vigorously in agreement. 'On with the glad rags!' added Max. 'I've booked the table.'

Even though she was sure that all this was unfair to Glenys and terribly unfair to Sebastian, too, it was with a fast-beating heart that Amy dressed for her dinner date with Max. In her whole life he had never taken her out to dinner before, and it was all forbidden, all wrong. She knew that. He had no right to simply leave Glenys and take her out. He had no right to place Sebastian in this situation. But he wanted to be with her! Her heart sang with the words.

She forgave him for his neglect of this week, forgave him for everything, and when she walked downstairs, her blue ballerina-length dress swirling around her, her black hair a shining halo, her bright blue eyes alive with nervous excitement, Max stood at the bottom of the steps and smiled up at her, open admiration on his face.

It felt like the last night of her life, Amy thought as she sat across from him in the smart and dimly lit dining-room of the biggest hotel in the district. After this there was France, then a few more weeks and school began again. Before the next holiday Max would be married, lost to her for ever—and she loved him!

She talked brightly, keeping him laughing, hiding her growing misery, determined to live this night as if it were her last, determined that he would at least remember her with a smile. She was only tightening her own nerves to breaking point, and she knew it, but there was nothing she could do about it. Max simply smiled into her eyes, helped her to the food and wine, treating her with that old affection that had never gone since she was a child.

Finally she could not keep up the bright, sparky chatter any longer and she fell silent.

'Tell me your worst fears and forebodings,' Max said quietly, his eyes intently on her unhappy face.

'I—I feel guilty, that's all. I know that—that we're old friends and things like that, but we really shouldn't be here when Glenys is at Belmore House and . . .'

'Glenys is for Sebastian,' Max said quietly, taking her hand across the table and holding it firmly.

'But—but I don't understand! You're going to marry her! That house . . .'

'Did I ever say I was going to marry Glenys?' he asked, his eyes holding hers.

'No, no, I don't think so, but you let me believe . . .'

'You weren't paying enough attention to me,' he said softly, 'and in all fairness, I had this project going long before you came back to me.'

'I didn't come back to you,' Amy said swiftly, still defensive. 'Max, I don't follow all this!'

'Sebastian is crazy about Glenys,' he explained, 'and she feels the same way too, but you know what they're like. It would be hilarious if it weren't poor old Seb. I decided to take a hand, bring them together. You did rather force my hand, because I imagined Seb was getting a bit too friendly with you and I blew my top. Tonight, however, is all part of the plan. Tonight he's on his own for the first time, sink or swim.'

'You should have told him!'

'And have him collapse with nerves? Not likely!' He smiled at her warmly. 'Now, will you help me to plan my house?'

CHAPTER SIX

AMY couldn't quite take it in, but a weight had lifted from her heart. Max was not philandering with her and intending to marry Glenys!

'The drawing-room is so sunny. It needs greys and blues,' she said a little breathlessly. 'I loved that room. It's such a happy house, Max. Oh, and the bedroom over it wants to be shades of pink and cream, a deep pink carpet.'

'Hold it!' he laughed. 'That room, I intend to have for myself. You'll get me a reputation with the builders.'

Amy blushed, falling silent. She still imagined herself in the house with Max, and his amused interruption had been like a reproof.

'Let's dance,' he said quietly, still watching her intently. 'Now that you know I'm not getting married, you can safely dance with me.'

She stood as he moved her chair, simply melting into his arms, moving with perfect grace, following his steps with ease.

'This is a treat,' he murmured, 'you actually dance as you walk, lightly and perfectly.'

'I don't think you should praise me too much,' she joked shakily. 'It goes to my head.'

'I couldn't praise you too much,' he said, deeply quiet. 'I can't ever find the words to describe you. I have to cast you in bronze—it's the only way I can express how beautiful you are.'

He moved her closer until her legs were against his, her

head against his chest, and his hands were warm and strong, caressing her hair. Everything in her cried out to him, wanting him, loving him, and he tilted her face, seeing the expression she had no time to hide.

'Maybe we should go?' Max's eyes held hers and she nodded, unable to speak, her lips suddenly dry, so dry that her tongue came out with an anxious secrecy to moisten them, her teeth biting into her lower lip as he swung her to the door without a further word.

It was no better in the car, and it was some time before Amy realised that they were not, in fact, on the way home. They were driving along by the sea, the moonlight brilliant on the water.

'Oh, how beautiful!' she exclaimed softly, and Max stopped the car at once, turning off the lights and opening the door.

'Let's walk,' he said abruptly, coming to help her out. She could feel the tension radiating from him, so much so that he never touched her, and she climbed the dunes, her sandals in her hand, the warm breeze blowing her dress around her as she ran as she had run years ago, barefoot on the pale sands.

It was different now, though. There was a different excitement. The moon struck like a shaft of light across the water, the breeze lifted her hair and her flowing skirts, the night was warm and Max was no longer her comfortable companion. He wanted her. The tension in him reached out to her even here when he was not even close, and the ecstasy of the knowledge filled her with joy. He must love her! It was too much to imagine that he could feel as he so clearly did and not love her too! Amy danced along the sand, brilliantly alive in the moonlight, ready to run into the sea and drown with the excitement that filled her.

Max caught her at the water's edge, grasping her wrist and swinging her towards him.

'You're crazy!' he said in a vibrant voice. 'You need a keeper!'

'You, Max!' she breathed, looking up at him, her eyes brilliant in the moonlight. 'You're my keeper!'

Max stared down into her upturned face, seeing the temptation there. His eyes, too, were alive with moonlight, a passion that was scarcely controlled blazing in him, and he pulled her close, his hands tightly possessive on her slender hips as she wound her arms around his neck.

'Oh, God!' he breathed thickly. 'Amy, you take my breath away!'

She was eager and alive in his arms, her blood racing with joy as he moulded her to him, his desire very obvious, and his lips burned into her, making no allowances now, parting her lips and plundering the sweetness inside like a man dying from hunger.

He swung her high into his arms and she lay there passively, her head thrown back, her arms wide, the silver sandals swinging from her hand.

'Where are we going?' It was like a dream, a dream she had dreamed and never hoped to dream again.

'You know where we're going!' Max said almost roughly, and she did. It was the same place where he had kissed her for the first time, almost the same hollow, as far as she could tell, and Max lifted her from the soft sand to put his dinner-jacket there for her head and shoulders. Then, before allowing her to sink back, he immediately pulled her into his arms.

There was no waiting in him. He wanted to kiss her, to hold her, and he came to her swiftly, overwhelming her with a desire that was feverish in its intensity. His mouth moved hotly over her skin, returning over and over to taste her lips. His hands were restless on her, those same hands, that could fashion her as a beautiful figurine, that could carve out marble that was ten feet high, that were strong and powerful, now traced her body with delight.

'You're beautiful, perfect! You bewitch me!' he murmured against her skin, his hands tracing the taut beauty of her breasts. He slid the dress from her shoulders, leaving her breasts white and perfect in the moonlight, their rosy peaks darkened by the night. 'Are you cold, darling?' But he did not wait for a reply; his head lowered and his lips nuzzled against her, drawing the hard peak into the warmth of his mouth.

'Max! Max!' It was no protest this time, but a wild cry of joy, and he recognised it, his hand moving to the smooth planes of her stomach as she cradled him against her.

'I want you, Amy!' he groaned, when at last his mouth hovered over hers again, and his hand moved to take possession of her throbbing breast. He kissed her lingeringly, deeply, his hands roaming over her until she was wild in his arms, only his weight keeping her still.

'We've got to go!' he gasped when the pain inside her had grown into a crescendo of desire.

'No!' Amy clung to him tightly, her face filled with rapture in the bright moonlight, her body twisting beneath the hands that still fondled her.

'We must—I can't keep my hands off you! Have mercy on me, sweet Amy. Tell me to stop!'

'I don't want to—I can't!' Her eyes were overbright, frantic, and he cupped her face in his hands, suddenly ferocious.

'Are you a virgin, Amy?' She stared at him, momentarily shocked by his rough demand, and he tightened his hands, his body heavily across her. 'Tell me!'

'Yes,' she gasped, fear racing inside her. 'But it doesn't make any difference, because I . . .'

'It makes a difference to me!' said Max with a soft violence. 'You're mine! Nobody else can have you!'

He loved her! Her heart was singing as she pulled his head down to her, raining kisses on his face, her body eager and soft.

'We must go! Don't you know what this is doing to me?'

'Yes!' she whispered triumphantly, moaning with pleasure when his lips caught hers again, taking control.

It seemed he could not stop now, and neither could she. Everything inside her cried out to belong to him, and when his hand slid over the smooth and silken skin of her thigh to move across her hips she waited with a breathless fear that he would stop, her body jerking in pained delight when his hand moved beneath the lacy top of her briefs to the warm source of her desire.

'Don't leave me!' The words seemed to be forced from her dry lips, and Max groaned his vibrant protest against her mouth.

'One of us must be wise!' He moved closer fiercely. 'How can I be wise and sensible when I want to make love to you so much?'

Amy couldn't answer, she was burning all over, aching to belong to him, and as he moved, sighing deeply and cradling her in his arms, she began to cry softly. 'Don't, darling!' Max murmured, in a despair of his own.

'I—I wanted y-you!' She hid her face in his shoulder and he held her tightly, rocking her against him.

'Don't make me feel worse than I already do,' he begged

in a driven voice. 'Hurting you is the last thing I ever intended.'

'You don't want me!' she accused tearfully, and he pulled her to her feet, holding her so tightly that she cried out.

'I want you too damned much, that's the whole trouble!' he grated violently, and the knowledge of that had to content her.

The house was dark when they reached home. It was much later than Amy had thought, but it was for the best. She could not have faced anyone the way she felt now, and she was sure her love for Max was written across her face for all to see. Certainly, he must have seen it as he left her at her door with a quick and gentle kiss, and the night was stretching before her endlessly, because she knew that sleep would not come for hours.

Max was to take her to the station the next day, and when she presented herself for breakfast he was already there with Aunt Joan. Everyone else, it seemed, had finished and she knew Bernice was already packing to take her little brood home.

'You look tired, Amy,' said Aunt Joan with a close look at her. 'I've never seen you look tired before.'

'I think I must be out of condition,' Amy muttered, knowing that her face was flushed and uneasy. 'I must start running again as soon as possible—that sprain quite put me off stride.'

Her aunt didn't look too convinced, and Amy knew she was a very astute woman. She saw her eyes move to Max's strained face and could almost hear her aunt's mind working. She could sense a growing shock in her too, and it did nothing to ease her own mind.

This morning was not as happy as she had thought it would be. Max's eyes had devoured her as she came into the room, but there was a look in them that she had never seen before, and she recognised it as guilt. He was regretting last night, regretting the whole thing, his conscience biting into him, and it could be for one reason only—he didn't love her.

Amy's own mind was not any too easy, either. In the beauty of the night, in his arms, it had been easy to forget everything. This morning, though, it was not easy at all. It was not in Amy's character to take things lightly, although she acted the part well. She had been speaking the truth when she had told Max that she felt deeply. She did, especially about Max. He had laughed when she had described her ideas about the bedroom, telling her it was to be his bedroom, and she realised sadly that he had wanted her, nothing more. They had always been close. She had come back into his life and he had wanted her. It was eating away at him, and she could do nothing to prevent her own feelings from showing when he looked at her.

'I'll pack.' She left the table abruptly, and Max called that he was ready when she was. It only remained to say goodbye to Sebastian as he left for work looking rather more light-hearted than usual, to hug the children and Bernice, and then she was ready, standing in her room with a sinking heart as she heard them all go down the stairs.

Could she ever come here again? Would Max love her? She moved to the door with her suitcase, seeing the closed door of his room, and a great desire surged through her to see the small figurine that he had done when she was a child. She had never seen it since that day in his studio, when she had cried with shame at her clumsiness and he had comforted her and shown her the beautiful image of herself.

Her actions were unforgivable and she knew it, but she had to look. There was nobody upstairs now and she ran lightly along to Max's room, opening the door softly and stepping inside.

Her regret was instantaneous. This was too overpoweringly Max. The smell of his aftershave, the feeling of his presence, his sweater on a chair—the whole room was Max, as if he stood here looking at her. She turned swiftly to the chest—and all her feelings focused into one great surge of shock.

The figurine was there, the one he had first done, as bright and perfect as it had been on the day she had first seen it. As she had half expected, the latest one was there, too, the leaping, carefree figure so perfectly executed that it almost had movement. But her shock was the photographs. He had kept the ones he had taken to use in the studio, and they were in silver frames, the very best one enlarged to a head-and-shoulder portrait, and Amy saw her own childhood's face smiling out at her. The ones Max had got from the newspapers were there too, framed, a permanent record of her win in Frankfurt. It was like a shrine, and it did not please her, it made her skin cold.

She never knew he was there until his arms wound around her waist and he pulled her back against him.

'Do you care to explain this intimate intrusion?' he murmured against her hair.

'I—I'm really sorry, Max. I had this great whim to see the figurine, and I know it's unforgivable, but . . .'

'But you know I'll forgive you,' he finished for her.

Foolishly, she felt endangered. He was so big, so strong,

and the sight of the photographs had unnerved her. She was trembling and he felt it, his arms tightening as he turned her back to look at the chest with its array of things he had called his treasures.

'You—you kept the photographs!' It was only a whisper, but it was accusing, and Max laughed softly, his lips brushing her hair.

'I kept the photographs,' he agreed. 'As you can see, you're an obsession, my only one.'

'I—I'm alive! I don't want to be an obsession, Max.'

'But you are.' He turned her in his arms, his eyes narrowed on her pale face. 'It frightens you, doesn't it? You're trembling in my arms like you were last night, but this time it's from fear.'

'Why should I be afraid?' asked Amy as spiritedly as her lips would allow, and he smiled into her eyes.

'Only you know that. Would you feel better if I destroyed them all, sold the figurines?'

'No!' She hated the thought of anyone else seeing her like that. It was secret to her and Max, something that had always been secret.

'Well now, that, if I'm not mistaken, is called contrariness.'

'I don't want to be an obsession to you, Max,' she got out breathlessly, her eyes locked with his, and his hand came to cup her face, his other arm tightly around her.

'What do you want to be—to me?'

'I don't know.' It was a lie and she knew it. She wanted to love him for ever, to be with him. She wanted his love, the love he would give to a woman who was alive and real. She wanted no obsession, no passing desire.

'It's time to go,' Max said quietly, watching her closely,

seeing the feelings race across her expressive face. 'I'll say my goodbyes here.'

And she was locked in his arms, his lips on hers, surrounded by warmth and tenderness; but deep inside she knew that Max had stepped back, back behind the wall of his strength. She no longer had the power to lure him as she had last night. With a graceful ease he had distanced himself from her, leaving her between two worlds, the carefree world of childhood when he had walked like a giant through her days, and the world of the moonlight and the sea when he had unleashed his passion on her, making her more of a woman than she had ever been before.

The moments with him flew by. Her aunt was coming home later in the week, seeing no need to hurry when Amy would be in France, and after a whole barrage of last-minute instructions they were off to the station.

Max did not say a word until they had placed her luggage in a first class compartment and Amy was standing on the platform, miserable and uneasy, waiting for the train to leave.

'When will I see you again?' He looked down at her, his voice low, and she hastily looked away, her eyes along the length of the train, her heart heavy with love for him.

'I don't know. School starts very soon after we get back, in a couple of weeks or so. I have things to do. Maybe if you're in London.'

'Go to Paris with me. When you come back from this trip, re-pack your bag with something suitable and fly straight back to Paris with me for the weekend.'

'I can't! I don't know what you mean.'

'You do, Amy.' Max moved closer, shielding her from the other passengers who waited in a desultory manner for their trains, unaware that Amy's life was being changed beyond recall by the handsome man who watched her with alert grey eyes.

'You—you're asking me to—to have an affair with you?' She couldn't believe this was Max, *her* Max, who had been her idol.

'We're already deep into a heated affair, I think, after last night,' he murmured softly, his hand coming to stroke her face. 'I want you with me, Amy. Just you and I, alone.'

'I can't!' The train gave a juddering sigh, doors slammed and she hurried to escape, her feelings a bewildering mixture of pain, excitement, disappointment and fear. 'I've got to go.'

'When you get back, I'll be there!' he said determinedly, holding on to her hand. 'I'll be waiting to take you with me!'

Amy pulled away and dived on to the train, hardly daring to look through the carriage window as the train left the platform. It was Max standing there—Max with silver-grey eyes that watched her with a hungry burning look that made her heart leap. He raised his hand, but she was powerless to acknowledge his farewell, her eyes blue and bewildered, locked with his until he was out of sight.

Paris was hot, perfect weather. The small hotel where they stayed was filled with the school party, every room taken. This was very unfortunate, according to Clive, as it gave the children no chance to mix with the French people who otherwise might have been there. About to enquire if he would have preferred to have the party spread all over Paris, Amy changed her mind and held her tongue. She could not even find the energy nowadays to have a good argument.

Distress about Max had left her dull-eyed and totally lacking her normal sparkle. She was not really interested in the children, and this added to her feeling of guilt. All the time her mind was on Max, trying to sort out her very mixed feelings.

What would she do if he really was there waiting for her when she landed back in England? Did she have the courage to say no, to remind herself that he felt only desire? Would she let his unexpected and burning passion sweep her into a situation that would bring grief to more than herself?

Several times in her life she had mused about the idea of having an affair, but she had never pursued the idea. Love meant too much to a person like herself, and love meant Max. It was no longer a teenage passion. Her love for Max ate into her, changing her way of thinking. If he had loved her she would have been walking on air, but he merely wanted an affair, and it had shattered the whole core of her life.

It became clear that Clive had taken a very large hand in the Headmaster's organisation, as with mathematical precision sights were visited and crossed off, and Amy's spirits began to rise under this adversity. She managed several times to manoeuvre her own small party to the very back, signalling them then with a casual nod until they were well clear and able to pursue the more rewarding delights of the roadside café, the pavement artists and the lively crowds.

It was not unnatural that her own party grew as Clive's and the Headmaster's diminished, a fact that did not seem to penetrate the rather saintly mind of the Head, but which brought an angry glint to Clive's steely eyes.

'This is irresponsibility!' he chastised sternly. 'This is a cultural trip!'

'This is supposed to improve their French!' countered Amy, the light of battle in her eyes. 'My party challenges yours to a duel—French conversation against architectural structure!'

Clive was not amused and thereafter looked at her grimly. He reported her to the Headmaster too, who remonstrated with her mildly, to the fury of the pupils, who at seventeen felt the burden of Clive's cultural feast like a lead weight in the stomach. By the final day, Clive's popularity had reached zero, and he blamed Amy. He refused to speak to her at all.

'Ah, well,' she thought, 'it was time to bid Clive farewell, anyway.' She had definitely been sailing under false colours with Clive, pretending to like the things that he liked. She pretended nothing with Max. He was more than capable of dealing with her. He was big enough in every way to allow her room to breathe, to be herself. There would never be anyone like Max.

The timing was immaculate, she had to admit that. From the ferry to the school coach that was waiting on time, to the arrival back at school as a dropping-off place, everything went like clockwork, and she congratulated Clive.

'Attention to detail is the most important thing!' he said, somewhat mollified by her unexpected praise. 'You're just too impetuous, Amy. Still, I suppose that's to be expected. You even *look* impetuous!'

'Do I really?' She was standing in the school yard as the pupils left the bus and made their separate ways home, and Clive looked down at her with a certain rueful acceptance of her faults, which clearly were many.

Neither of them was aware of the tall man who approached, until he spoke almost in Amy's ear.

'What type of impetuosity has she been guilty of?' Amy swung round, her heart lurching at the deep sound of Max's voice, and Clive looked at him with surprise. It was not often that a man like this appeared in this area; in fact it was the first time ever.

'Er—this is Maxwell St Clair,' Amy said quickly, then introduced Clive.

'We did enjoy your work at the exhibition, didn't we, Amy?' Clive said enthusiastically, adding with a laugh, 'But then I suppose you've heard that already, as Amy knows you so well.'

'Yes, Amy knows me well,' Max said softly. 'Nice to have met you. We have to hurry now.'

His arm came round Amy's shoulders with a possessive tightness, and Clive looked startled for a second before turning away, his mind already back on his own affairs. It was clear he felt a certain relief that Amy was being so possessively claimed.

'How did you know . . .?' Amy began as they walked towards Max's car, a car that looked excessively expensive to be parked at the school gates.

'Attention to detail, as your wayward swain remarked. I enquired!' He glanced down at her. 'You look tired. Has it been a drag?'

'In a word, yes!' Amy conceded with a sigh. 'I got into trouble, too, for taking my group to more exciting things than churches and museums.'

'Where did you take them?' Max stopped by the car and smiled down at her.

'Cafés!'

'Ah, the impetuosity!' He was suddenly serious. 'Now,

are you going to go back there with me, to see Paris as it really is, just you and I?'

'I can't, Max!' She looked away, but he turned her face back to his.

'Look at me as you break my heart, *please!*'

'I can't go! What would Aunt Joan think?'

'She'll think what she thought when she saw us together at the breakfast table, I imagine,' Max said quietly. 'You're not particularly good at hiding your feelings and, where you're concerned, neither am I.'

'I've always thought you were wonderful, Max,' she said forlornly, and he looked at her seriously.

'But now you doubt it?'

'I've never had an—an affair before. I don't want to be hurt.'

'I've hurt you already, I think. How you feel finally is my only vindication. Come with me, Amy!' he said deeply.

She looked up into his face, her eyes deeply blue, searching his expression for some sign, some comfort, and she imagined she saw a sort of love. Certainly, there was more than desire, but then he had cared for her for years.

'I'll come.' She said it quickly, before her head gained control of her heart, and Max bent to kiss her swiftly and sweetly.

'I'll take you home and then pick you up in three hours. It will give you time to pack and rest a bit. The flight leaves at five. We'll be in our hotel in good time for dinner.'

'You booked? Suppose I'd said no? Were you so sure of me?' Amy asked bitterly.

'No,' he said softly. 'It's a matter of living on hope. I've been doing that for the six days you were away. If you'd said no, then I think I would have gone alone and imagined you there. I do a lot of that lately.'

As he helped her into the car, there were tears in her eyes, and he was not mistaken about the cause.

'Save your pity, wench,' he said with a short laugh. 'Just remember that I'm the villain.' Amy shook her head, unable for the moment to speak. Max was not the villain. He just didn't feel for her what she felt for him, and he imagined a few nights of love would heal the wounds inside her.

Aunt Joan was horrified.

'You're going to Paris for the weekend—with Max?' she stared at Amy with worried eyes. 'My dear child, you must tell him you can't go!'

'I want to go, Aunt Joan. Please understand.'

'I understand perfectly well,' her aunt said quietly, 'and I'm neither shocked nor bewildered, but this is Max! He means too much to you, Amy. He always has.'

'If he didn't, I wouldn't be going,' Amy said with painful honesty.

'Amy, you'll be so badly hurt!'

'I'm hurt now,' Amy told her in a whisper. 'At least I'll have something to remember.'

She was ready in good time. She didn't want Max to have to come in for her. Her aunt would not speak to him, she had already said so, and Amy realised that the destruction was already spreading. Nothing would ever be the same. More lives than her own were due to be shattered, but Max had called her and she had to go. She would run to his arms if he stood in hell.

Max looked closely at her as she went to the car, taking her suitcase and stowing it away before he joined her.

'You're very unhappy.' He was not asking her. He knew her too well to be mistaken.

'Aunt Joan says she—she'll never speak to you again.'

He nodded grimly, his eyes on the traffic.

'I expected that. I'd have been disappointed if she'd happily faced the thought of you coming away with me. She's spent many years looking after you. In many ways you've been more of a responsibility than if you'd been her own child. She carries a double responsibility for you—she only holds you in trust, as it were.'

'And now I've shattered everything! Now she'll never again go to Belmore House, in case she sees you! She won't feel the same any more about anything!'

Amy clenched her hands together, gripping them so tightly that they looked white and dead.

'Do you want to go back? Do you want to tell her that you've changed your mind?'

'No.' She hung her head in despair. 'The damage is already done. Whether or not I go back, she's going to remember that you asked me and that I wanted to come.'

'Do you?' Max's voice was very quiet, but she could feel tension in him as he waited for her answer.

'Yes, you know I do. If I didn't, I wouldn't be here now. I've never, ever been made to do something I didn't want to do. I'm much too bad-tempered to allow anyone to—to talk me into anything.'

'Spirited, Amy,' Max corrected quietly, 'not bad-tempered. Your spirit is part of your great charm. You're like a sunny day, the white foam on the crest of a wave, wild, clean, breathtaking.'

Amy turned her head away, looking out of the window. Somehow, the words no longer described how she felt inside; she felt crushed, weighed down with guilt, trapped by her great love, by her desire to be with Max in any circumstances.

He swung the car into the entrance of an expensive hotel, getting out and helping her out too, locking the doors.

'Where are we going?' She could hear the panic in her own voice. She wanted to cling to the door of the car. Was this where Max was taking her? Were they going no further than here?

'My hotel,' he said evenly. 'I've been staying here. I want to collect my case, and I rather think they'll be expecting me to pay the bill. They were getting it ready as I left to pick you up.' He took her arm firmly and led her inside the rather imposing foyer. 'I also think you could do with a drink.'

'I'd love a cup of tea!' Amy was so giddy with relief that she felt almost hysterical. How she would be when they got to Paris, to *the* hotel, she dared not think.

'A brandy, I imagine, would serve the purpose better,' said Max grimly, leading her to the guests' lounge and ordering without any further ado.

Amy sat beside him, almost huddled up, realising she was making an utter fool of herself. Did a man want someone like this with him? Was he feeling he had kidnapped her? Looking at him, she would have said he was feeling nothing at all. He spoke little, and the things he said were so bland, so polite, that it might have been a stranger who sat beside her, not a man who wanted her so passionately that he was prepared to alienate his family to take her with him.

And that was exactly what would happen, Amy knew. She could not imagine Aunt Dorothy taking this lightly, nor Bernice. She could see Sebastian's shocked face when he found out, and although Benedict St Clair, because of his work and his duties in London, knew her least of all, he would not expect this from his oldest son. They would look on her, too, with different eyes; even Bernice would do that.

Her nerves were as tight as the strings of a violin, singing with tension and fright. All that the brandy did was make her feel more depressed, and when Max came back from paying his bill and took her arm, looking at his watch with a brisk and impatient gesture, she felt that all the other people in the room knew exactly where she was going—and why.

CHAPTER SEVEN

Amy had another brandy on the plane, and then another. She ordered them herself, catching the steward's eye as he passed, smiling at him brilliantly, like a confirmed alcoholic. Max said nothing. He neither approved nor disapproved, and although the brandies did not actually make her drunk, they anaesthetised her to a certain extent. They also made her feel very light on her feet, so much so that Max had to hold her very firmly by the arm as they left the airport and went by taxi to the hotel.

She hung back while Max signed the register, well aware that the clerk was looking at her very hard, an assessing look that made her colour flare. As they were just in time for dinner, the luggage was taken up for them and they were ushered straight into the dining-room.

She was hungry, she realised that, and the food looked delicious, but she could do little more than pick at it, in spite of Max's care and attention for her. Her mind was numb, frozen with fear, and there was nothing she could do about it. This was not going to be like any other time that Max had held her. There would be no romance in it, it would be coldblooded. They were here in Paris, far away from anyone who knew them, about to embark on an affair that would alter her life and Max's life, whether he realised it or not.

'Are we going to go out and see the sights?' she asked, too brightly, as they drank coffee, the meal finished. Her voice was too loud, she could even hear that herself.

'I think we'll leave that until tomorrow. We'll make an early start. There really is no need to go back until Monday, so tonight we'll get an early night,' said Max with an easy quiet that sounded to Amy's ears like the approach of doom.

He went for the key and came back to her, motioning her into the lift and smiling down at her, as she told herself over and over, in a rush of panic, that this was Max, that she loved him, that he had never been anything but kind and gentle. It did little to calm her, though, and when he stopped and put the key into the door she felt ready to faint with panic.

Like a figure made of stone, she walked into the room as he switched on the lights.

'Comfortable,' he decided after a swift look round; Amy had not dared to look anywhere. 'The bathroom is there, and here's the service button.' He methodically showed her everything, but she saw nothing at all, and when he took her hand, her fingers were icy and stiff.

'Here's your key,' he said softly. 'Don't forget to lock your door, and if you want anything, I'm just next door. Get an early night and tomorrow we'll see Paris.'

Amy just stared at him, unable to quite take in what was happening.

'Are you all right, Amy?' He looked at her with concern. 'If you want a tray of tea, I'll get it sent up to you.'

'But—but aren't you staying here in—in this room too . . .' Her eyes were dazed, over-large in her white face, and he cupped her cheeks in his hands, smiling down at her.

'My dear Miss Tremaine, that's the most wonderful invitation I've ever received in my life, but no, I have a room of my own. This is your room, booked in your own name.'

'But—but the man at the desk . . . he was staring at me as if—as if . . .'

'Sweet Amy, you're beautiful! This is Paris! Naturally he was staring at you. It was only this morning that you left the city. Didn't you notice men staring at you during the week?'

Amy shook her head numbly. She hadn't, but then of course she hadn't been feeling guilty, hadn't been filled with panic. She was not expected to share a room with Max. He knew she was frightened and tired. Tears pricked at her eyes and she blinked rapidly, lowering her head.

'I'm a real pain, Max. I realise that,' she whispered, but he laughed, a quiet, gentle sound deep in his throat.

'You're an angel,' he said softly. 'Goodnight, Amy.'

Too giddy with relief to think clearly, Amy went to bed. She reasoned it all out in the morning, though. This was not just any man she had come to Paris with, this was Max. Max knew her, had been fond of her all her life. There was no way that he would force his attentions on her when she was as tight with anxiety as she had been the night before.

So far, she had melted into his arms every time he had touched her; her reactions the night before must have been very obvious, and he was prepared to wait. As to the room, it was a matter of discretion. Max was not an uncouth boy, he must have had affairs before; he was sophisticated, rich, famous, naturally he would not relish any sordid and cheap affair. She had it all thought out, but it did nothing to still the beat of her heart when he came to escort her down to breakfast.

They had come to see Paris, and they did just that. Max knew the city well, spoke French fluently and knew Amy so well that everything he had to show her was a little bit of magic. He knew every bridge over the Seine, every place where artists performed in the streets, jugglers, acrobats, singers. They became part of the happy, excited crowds, and Amy relaxed and blossomed, a little of her spirit returning.

With her hand in Max's, the sun hot and strong, the day stretching before them, there was nothing to fear and everything to enjoy. It was with the coming of darkness that her face tightened again with anxiety. She was not so apprehensive as she had been the night before, but as they ate dinner at the hotel she found that conversation was not as easy as it had been during the bright day.

Max left her at her door this time, his smile warm and affectionate, and though she leaned against the locked door when he had gone, her knees shaking, she felt the stirrings of a very small but very definite disappointment. Since they had been in Paris he had not kissed her once; he had been so pleasantly formal as to almost be at the stage of shaking her hand.

Sunday was exactly the same. Here, Max insisted that she visit Notre-Dame, a place she had skipped wilfully on her trip here with the school. At night, too, there was a variation; they ate out, and she knew this was their last night in the city. This, then, was the night.

Her worries were confirmed when Max opened her door for her and escorted her inside. Her alarm grew as he walked towards her with a determined look on his face.

'Max,' she began timidly, her whole body tight with

agitation as he folded her into his arms.

'Shh! Be still, Amy.' He tilted her face, his lips claiming hers instantly, drowning her little moans of fear, his arms gathering her to him as if she was a frightened child. There was something about the kiss that absolutely forbade excitement. Max was kissing her! Max was setting the tone!

She relaxed, and he allowed her to seek the warmth of his body as she nestled as close as she could get, but he was not in any way allured by her. There was no desire in him. When he lifted his head, she had been thoroughly and masterfully kissed, but the air was not electric, the room was not spinning.

'As this is our last night here,' he said slowly, his eyes roaming over her bewildered face, 'I figured it was safe to kiss you goodnight before I go to my room.' He smiled and kissed the tip of her nose. 'The flight leaves at noon, but I want to do a little shopping before we go, so get up reasonably early.'

With that, he simply walked to the door.

'Max!' Her rather anxious cry stopped him and he turned, his face questioning.

'I—I thought you—you wanted me. I suppose I've put you off—I mean, I know how I've been. I realise that . . .' Amy stopped, bewildered by the look on his face. 'Don't you want me any more, Max?'

He walked back, cupping her face in his strong, warm hands.

'Only urgently,' he said with a soft laugh. 'I didn't bring you to Paris to make love to you, though. There are many things you don't yet understand, and, as I told you before, it will keep.'

* * *

With a contrariness taking the place of her fear, Amy sat on the flight back beside a seemingly happy and contented Max. She had presents in her bag: perfume, a silk scarf that she had thought outrageously expensive and, to her great shame, a gold bracelet that had stunned her both by its beauty and its cost.

'But I didn't do anything!' she had said in a subdued voice, and he had laughed at her worried face.

'I've been buying you presents since you were in ankle socks, Amy. I fail to see the difference.'

'I'm not in ankle socks now,' she retorted, suddenly angry, 'and it *is* different!'

'It was never my intention to buy you, darling,' Max said quietly, and her blushes silenced them both.

Aunt Joan was stiff with worry when she saw Amy. She had made no attempt to come to the door as Max had stopped, and he had grinned at the closed door, handed Amy her bag, kissed her on her cheek and driven off. She felt utterly foolish, childish and cheated.

'Amy!' Aunt Joan took one look at her face and sat down with a thump, her worst fears confirmed. 'Oh, my dear! I told you how it would be!'

'And you were wrong!' snapped Amy, throwing her jacket at the settee in an attempt to relieve her feelings. 'He treated me like—like an idiot child! He never laid a hand on me. He only kissed me once!'

Her aunt's face was aglow with thankfulness, as if she had been delivered from the devil.

'Oh, thank you, God!' she said softly, her hands clasped tightly in her lap.

'Aunt Joan, you just don't understand!' Amy protested

rather tearfully, but she got only a wider smile.

'My dear, I'm not at all senile. I should think that one day, you'll understand, too.'

Max came to tea. He simply invited himself and arrived without warning, a gift from Paris for her aunt and a rather smug look about him that Amy found vastly irritating. One result, though, was that his instant arrival and his smug, amused attitude did more to restore her to her rightful mind than an army of psychiatrists would have been able to do. In a word, she was annoyed and it showed. Max was not at all perturbed, and when he left he simply patted her cheek, right under Aunt Joan's nose!

Of course, it gradually dawned on Amy that Max was simply playing with her emotions, treating her with wry amusement just because he had felt a sudden burst of desire for her and had flirted with her outrageously. She supposed the trip to Paris had been his method of straightening things out, making her feel easy and able to visit her friends in Northumberland without embarrassment. There could be no doubt in his mind that he had gone too far, had led her on to the point of surrender, and this was his way of coping with things. No other explanation seemed to fit, although she sat up for most of the night tearing herself apart with the effort of trying to understand.

After five years of absence, she had walked back into his life, even walking all over his plans for Seb, and she knew how irritating she could be; she was really an expert at putting her foot into things. Hadn't she, after all, nearly spoiled everything by encouraging Sebastian, right under the horrified gaze of Glenys? It was more than likely that

Max had set out to take her right out of the picture, and it had simply gone too far. After all, he was a very virile man.

Amy had always been able to pull herself up by sheer determination, and next day saw the greatest effort that she had ever made.

'Good morning!' She breezed downstairs and kissed Aunt Joan on the cheek, her bright happiness quite stopping her aunt in her tracks as she prepared breakfast.

'Are you all right, Amy, dear?' Her aunt looked closely at her, and here was the first hurdle. Anyone who had been scrutinised by her aunt had been scrutinised by an expert; nothing escaped her.

'Naturally! I'm going for my run. Save me a good breakfast!'

She let herself out into the bright air of the day and began to run at once, keeping her mind beautifully blank, keeping to the same route, falling easily into the well controlled rhythm of an experienced athlete. So far, so good. Her mind moved to the rhythm, chanting an incantation to ward off pain. 'Anybody can do anything, anybody can do anything.' The moment his name came into her mind, she shut it out, her blue eyes bright and alert, her hand raising briefly from time to time, as people who knew her called out greetings.

She was safe in her usual role, and if Max came she would continue to play her part. She would play it until she was back in the role securely. She had been happy until she had gone up to Northumberland and seen him again. She did not need Max. She ran on and shut his name from her mind.

He was just driving up as Amy ran back along the street

later. She saw his car and her heart almost stopped, but there was no hiding; in her bright red track suit she was certainly conspicuous, and anyway, seeing him was part of the test. Those silver-grey eyes saw very deeply what was in her mind and heart. She simply ran on, and he got out of his car and watched her as she approached, his eyes just a little wary.

'Oh, hi!' Amy stopped and put her hands on her knees, bending and taking deep breaths. 'Gosh, I'm out of condition! I'll have to do this twice a day in future until I feel all right again. It wouldn't do to appear in school for the new term looking a wreck.'

'Bright and cheerful this morning, I see,' he murmured, his eyes on her red track suit and then on the brilliant blue of her eyes against her black hair. 'Definitely bright, anyway,' he added, with a curious look at her.

'Surely you know that I'm always bright and cheerful, Max? Are you coming in? I still haven't had breakfast.' She opened the door and he walked in behind her, his face still and thoughtful.

'Max is here!' Amy managed to call out to her aunt, in exactly the same way she had called when she was a child and Max had unexpectedly dropped in during one of his visits to London. The effect was the same, too. Her aunt appeared with her face wreathed in smiles, although she did give Amy a very sharp and searching look.

'I'm going to shower. I'll eat when I come down.' Amy dismissed Max as if he was a visitor for her aunt, and she never looked around to see how he was taking it. She could no longer afford to belong to Max in any way.

She was still winning when she came back downstairs, fresh and glowing, her hair blow-dried into a glorious, shining cap of blue-black perfection. She slid neatly into her seat at the table, ignoring the way that his eyes lingered over her petite figure in the buttercup-yellow dress.

'Now for the reward!' She helped herself to bacon, eggs and freshly made toast, smiling cheerfully at Max and beginning to tell Aunt Joan about the people who had called to her on her run.

'Oh, and Mrs Jones wants to know if she can borrow the recipe you demonstrated at the Ladies' Circle. I said you might take it round, or I will, if you like.'

She knew that apart from a bright smile she was ignoring Max. She knew, too, that her aunt was utterly mystified. Max was not! He watched her with that deep and possessive look that so devastated her, waiting for a break in her bright chatter before saying, 'I came to take you out for the day.'

'Oh, sorry, Max, but I really can't. I shall have to drive over to school and see to a few things. It's always necessary, you know. We really have to be ready for the new intake in September.'

'What things?' he asked with an amused gleam in his eyes.

'Too numerous to mention. I'll be most of the day, and then I have a few people to see.'

'Who?' Her aunt got up and went into the kitchen, leaving Amy to it.

'Various members of staff, things like that.' She drank her tea, cradling the cup in her hands, looking down at it.

'Being Head of Department must surely be an enormous and time-consuming responsibility,' observed Max as he took the cup from her hands and put it back on its saucer. 'Stop being an idiot, Amy!'

'I'm sure I don't know what you mean, Max.' She looked squarely at him, controlling her pulse rate by willpower, blushing when his eyes rested on the rapid rise and fall of her breasts.

'I'm here for four more days,' he told her quietly. 'I want to see you every day.'

'Oh? That's nice. Why?' She tossed her head, almost overdoing the act but just catching herself in time.

'I'll get up and beat you, Amy,' he threatened softly, his eyes a mixture of amusement and frustration.

'I should warn you, I did karate at college,' she said with a wild ferocity, and he actually laughed outright.

'You'd fit into my pocket, sweet Amy. It might be fun, though, to see you in action. Get your bag and hurry up, you're coming with me.'

'You should understand, Max, that you can't order me about!' Amy said hotly, seeing her victory slipping away. 'I really don't want to go anywhere with you.'

'Are you coming?' He got up and towered over her, his face threatening, and she got her bag.

Not that it made much difference. Max treated her like a small and amusing sister. Amy knew that her anxiety was making her a bit wild, but somehow she just could not help it. It was so very necessary to show him that she was no more involved than he was.

He seemed to be set on showing her London as he had shown her Paris, and she had to admit that, though she had lived here since she was small, he knew it as well as she did. There was a magic in seeing things with Max, listening to his voice, feeling the firm hand on her arm, and she knew that he was working hard at easing them both back into the way they had been with each other before all this had happened.

For three days, she was with him constantly. He was waiting for her each day as she came in from her run and he took her out for the rest of the day. Sometimes it was necessary to call in and change for dinner, and he talked quietly to her aunt as he waited. Each night, Aunt Joan disappeared discreetly to her bed after a suitable time spent chatting to Max, but when she did, Max said goodnight to Amy and left at once. Gradually, her initial suspicions were confirmed. Max was setting the scene for a return to normality. Glenys and Sebastian were happily going out together, he told her, and she knew that with his fit of madness over, Max wanted things as they had always been.

And it was impossible to resist him. Loving him as she did now, a tremendous blossoming of the steady love that had been there all her life, Amy slid into his ways again. If she could only have Max as a friend and companion, then that was what she would have to be content with. There would never be anyone else, she knew that for sure.

The last night, when Aunt Joan did her discreet disappearing act, Max stayed.

'Would you like some coffee?'

Suddenly, Amy was uneasy with him again. He was always so big, so powerful, filled with a driving energy that quite outshone her own, and here in an ordinary house, a small town house that was nothing like his great mansion in Northumberland, he seemed to grow in size.

'If you like.' He watched her with lazy grey eyes and she flushed deeply.

'That's no way to answer? Do you or do you not want coffee?'

'Come here!' He reached for her wrist and swung her towards him, catching her to him and looking down at her with a curious intensity in his eyes. 'You're so damned *tiny!*' he murmured, swinging her up into his arms.

He sat down and pulled her across his knee, and she went into a frenzy of wildly moving arms and legs, unable to shout as she would have liked to do because of her aunt sleeping upstairs.

'Let me go, Max! Just what do you think you're doing?' she muttered breathlessly, terrified by the growing excitement that she had worked so hard to banish for ever.

'Nothing I haven't done before.' He trapped her arms and legs quite easily by lifting her and holding her tightly to his chest. 'Tell me when you've finished, you little madwoman. I honestly don't want to do you any permanent damage, but you're so small that maybe you'll break into pieces.'

There was not a lot of future in battling physically with Max, and Amy changed her tactics, relaxing until he held her on his lap, his arms only loosely round her.

'We've always been such good friends, Max!' she appealed softly, looking down to avoid his eyes. 'We've been best friends.'

'I can't deny that,' he said reasonably, laughter in his voice.

'These—these few days have been quite like old times,' she murmured, looking up at him with bright and anxious eyes. 'I've really enjoyed them.'

'I'm so glad,' he assured her seriously, his eyes on her fascinating face.

'You—you're rather spoiling things now, though,' she told him quietly and carefully. 'Tomorrow you'll be going, and I really want to remember these nice friendly days.'

He was laughing quietly, and Amy fought hard to control her temper. He was off again, thinking that he could wind her around his finger when he had nothing else to do. She glared up at him and he threaded his fingers through her hair, holding her head tightly.

'Is the drama lesson over?' he enquired politely, lifting her face to his when she went into violent action again, and silencing her with his hard mouth.

'Max!' She tore her mouth away, but he came after her immediately, his eyes intent on her lips.

'Be quiet, you crazy child! I want to kiss you!'

His lips covered hers and all the fight went out of her. He only had to touch her, she only had to breathe in the scent of him, and she forgot everything else. His lips tasted her, soothed her and comforted her. His hands no longer needing to hold her in any control, as she wound her arms around his neck and simply gave up.

'Isn't this better than fighting, sweetheart?' he asked huskily. 'Don't you need this?' His lips trailed over her cheeks, along the slender column of her neck as his hands caressed her trembling body.

'In Paris and—and all week you've never . . .' She stopped abruptly as he caught her mouth in a deep and searching kiss, and when later her trembling told him to stop, he cradled her against him, his hands now only soothing.

'Maybe I've been courting you, darling Amy,' he said with tender mockery. 'Let's face it, these last three days

I've called on you and taken you out. I've brought you chocolates, wined and dined you, spent almost all my time with you. Didn't I do it right? I even paid my respects to your aunt.'

Amy looked up into his eyes and they were the same as ever, laughing down at her. The fire went out of the night.

Max stood, putting her gently on her feet and smoothing her tumbled hair.

'I'm going back tomorrow, so I won't see you. I'll ring you.' He kept his arm around her until he was at the door and then kissed her swiftly and gently. 'Goodnight, sweet Amy,' and he was gone, leaving Amy too dazed to really think.

She went to bed slowly, the trembling still in her limbs, the aching still inside, and her mind went over his words, over and over. Had he really meant it? Did he really care for her like that? How was it that, after years of knowing him as she knew herself, she now did not know him at all?

The next evening, she went to the theatre with Kitty. They had been promising themselves a night out for ages, and Kitty rang to say that she had tickets. Amy had thought it was Max, for one wild and happy moment, but maybe he was still driving north. She wasn't going to wait in and hang around the telephone, anyway.

It was really crowded and they had good seats, not expensive but well positioned because, as Kitty said with a breathless anticipation, half of the joy of coming to a show like this was looking at the wealthy in the better seats, spotting celebrities. She even got Amy doing it.

Amy saw Max as soon as he came in and her eyes just couldn't look away. He wasn't driving north, preparing to ring her, he was here, right here at this show—and he was not alone. Amy's heart grew heavy with pain at the sight of his companion, all his words of the previous night racing like small devils through her mind. Courting her! Why should he, when he was with this gorgeous creature?

She was tall and slim; a redhead—beautiful, glowing burnished hair that was piled on her head in fiery glory. Her clothes, her face, everything about her was exquisite, and Max had that same possessive hold on her arm that he had only seemed to have for Amy. Everyone knew her. She was stopped time after time, her smile beautiful as he paused to talk. They knew Max too—important-looking people who would not notice Amy if she suddenly did a cartwheel down the centre aisle. And her place in his life suddenly became crystal clear.

Only because of her aunt Dorothy had she been even a small part of his life. He had found her amusing, sweet and endearing. He had taken to her as a small and unusual entity in his already important life. The rest was as she had imagined it—and as to last night, hadn't he already told her that he was a philanderer?

She couldn't stop watching them, the way they stood with their heads together talking, the way they laughed. Max would not be talking to this sophisticated older woman as he had talked to her. This woman was not a lunatic, a crazy child, a madwoman! Amy saw nothing of the first part of the show, and when the lights rose for the interval she hardly dared to move. She did not want to go for a drink and risk bumping into them, but when she looked at the place where they had been, they were gone, and they did not return. She could imagine them in some expensive flat, Max with his powerful arms around the woman, no laughter in his voice as he spoke to her, their feelings so urgent that they had been forced to leave the theatre.

When she got home, Aunt Joan was still up.

'Oh, Max called,' she said smugly.

'Did he?' Amy asked, with a great attempt to drive the dull and lifeless sound out of her voice. 'Was he back in Northumberland, then?'

'He didn't say, dear, but I expect so,' her aunt said comfortably. 'He said he'd ring you tomorrow evening.'

From the woman's flat, no doubt, Amy thought miserably. Even before she went to bed, she knew for sure that she just couldn't stand it. She was beginning to break up inside, and she would have to do something drastic.

CHAPTER EIGHT

'I'M going to the cottage.'

Amy's announcement next morning had her aunt completely surprised, and she stopped her preparations for breakfast to stare at Amy with very suspicious eyes.

'Why? I thought you had lots to do at school?'

'Nothing that can't wait. You know I try to get down to the cottage twice a year, and so far I haven't been there at all. I've got two weeks left of my holiday and I just have this urge to get down to the cottage, to take *Bluebird* out.'

She began to help with breakfast, trying very hard to keep her face averted without being too obvious about it, and after a minute her aunt resumed her activities, though it was pretty certain that with the renewed action of her hands that prying brain had not stopped working.

'I can't come down with you, Amy,' she said a trifle anxiously. 'I've got too many things to do. There's a meeting of the Ladies' Circle this week, and then we're going on our annual next Monday.'

Amy nodded, smiling to herself. The 'annual' was a trip to the theatre, where all the ladies behaved as if they had never been there before. It was followed by a dinner at a West End hotel, something that Aunt Joan called a 'knees-up' but Amy was sure was a very dignified affair, having seen her aunt dress up to go more than once.

'I didn't think you would be, dear,' she said with a wide

smile. 'I'm glad, too. You only worry about me.'

'I'll worry even more when I'm not with you,' Aunt Joan said, obviously trying to put her off. 'It's a very dangerous sea there!'

'I know the sea! I was born and bred there,' Amy reminded her firmly. 'I know I've been here with you since I was a little girl, but I've been back every year. I haven't forgotten how to sail and I still have friends there. Jim Trehearne was doing up *Bluebird* for me at Easter. It should be in tip-top condition by now. They don't come any better than Jim. I'm really excited about it!'

'What shall I say if Max rings?' asked Aunt Joan with that quiet steadiness that she always used when dropping a spanner into the works.

'Tell him I'm out!' said Amy a little too sharply, taken off guard.

'For two weeks? He'll be down here like a rocket to see what's going on!'

'Why on earth should he?' snapped Amy, realising she was losing the advantage to her cunning relative. 'I've been going there all my life!'

'Don't beat about the bush, Amy!' her aunt said briskly. 'When you suddenly decided you had to come back to London before that trip to France with the school, Max was off like a shot, after you. He'll only do it again.'

'He happened to be in London at the time,' Amy said, sitting down and watching her breakfast intently. 'He merely called round to see me.'

She didn't quite catch what her aunt Joan said. It was one of those words she used at times of great irritation, a mixture of 'bosh!' and 'dash!' that meant nothing, but added up to an assessment of Amy's stupidity.

She let the matter drop, though, and it was not mentioned again until Amy was actually at the door, her car boot open ready for the two suitcases she had decided to take.

'If Max rings . . .'

'*When* Max rings . . .' her aunt corrected quickly, her face quite prim and her arms folded.

'I don't want you to tell him where I am,' Amy finished, with a steady look of her own.

'Have you ever been able to get the better of Max?' her aunt asked wryly, and when Amy shook her head she finished, 'Then what makes you imagine I can?'

'Because *you* are foxy!' Amy said with a grin, going out to the car. Not that Max would come down, if he had ever gone! He would be too busy taking up where he had left off, before he had been foolish enough to have this romantic interlude with her. She drove off with the feeling of having escaped something by the very skin of her teeth. She would have to recover. Everybody recovered, didn't they?

The drive to Cornwall was long, but Amy didn't mind that; she would need the car when she got there. Aunt Joan called it the back of beyond, and in a way she was quite right. The small fishing village where Amy had been born and had spent the first few happy years of her life had never changed. Tourists wandered in and out, but there was nothing here for them, really. There was no beach for miles. The cliffs dropped sheer to the sea and the tiny fishing harbour nestled in them, a small haven from a wild and dangerous sea. There were strong tides, dangerous undercurrents, and it was not a place recommended for the holidaymaker. Miles further down the coast there was wonderful surfing, the beaches were good and the sea less of a threat. They went there. It was only the dedicated few who came to Port Garvith.

It was always the same; each time she came here the years rolled away, and Amy was back in the strange and beautiful atmosphere of her father's land. Morgan Tremaine had spent the whole of his life here, married a girl from what he'd always called England, to emphasise that, to many, Cornwall was a land in itself. He had worked on the sea, lived by it and finally died in it with the wife he adored. If he were here now, what would he tell her to do? What would he think of Max? Would he remind her of the love Max had given her for so many years, or would he condemn him furiously for betraying her love now?

Amy stopped the car at the side of the road as she came to the entrance to the small fishing port. Beyond, the road fell away into the steep descent to the harbour itself, winding and clinging to the cliff until the harbour wall was reached. White houses clung there, too, their roofs at different and unusual angles that showed the age of the place but all tiled with the dour grey of Cornish slate.

The cottage where Amy had been born was among them, a small stone cottage that stood away from the rest, its back to the sea. From here she could see it, recognise its sturdiness. It had been built to withstand the weather, to stand four-square to the winds that blew across the land and bent the blackthorn into weird shapes. It was the cottage of a fisherman, the best there had been, a man with black hair and brilliantly blue eyes, his face tanned by the sun and the sea, his eyes reading the waves and currents as others read road maps. But it had taken him, even so, and her mother.

Tears that she had not shed for them for many years came into her eyes, and she got back in the car, impatient with herself. Morgan Tremaine had never held with sentimentality; he had been too alive to have any patience with death, and his beloved Prudence was with him, anyway. There was only Amy left.

She was feeling sorry for herself, and that could stop right now! She let in the gears and began the descent that would bring her to the gates of her own cottage, a place that had never been sold, a place that Aunt Joan and Aunt Dorothy had grimly held on to, her only legacy, that they had guarded even when times were hard and the money from its sale would have been a great help. And now she needed it as a refuge, a refuge from Max.

Her arrival did not go unnoticed and, even before she had got her bags inside the cottage, Jim Trehearne came sauntering across the road from his cottage almost opposite.

'Never knew you were coming, Amy girl! We could have been airing the place out. Thought you were giving us a miss this year!'

'Not likely!' Amy stopped and turned to smile at him. He was in his early fifties, his hair greying, his well rounded figure made larger by the dark blue fisherman's jersey that he almost invariably wore. He had been a handsome thirty-year-old when he had sailed on her father's boat.

'Place'll be damp. Stay with us tonight.'

'OK.' Amy was secretly glad of his invitation. Now that she was here, she didn't want to be alone. She didn't want to sit and brood about Max, and the Trehearne household was lively. 'I'll get the bedding aired, light a fire and come over.'

'Right, the woman will be pleased!' The woman was his wife, and Amy always hid a smile when he referred to her like that. The woman had snapping black eyes, a sharp tongue and a very pointed sense of humour. She matched him pound for pound in weight, too, and ruled the household with a firm but friendly hand.

'*Bluebird*'s ready,' Jim remarked casually, making it sound as if he had simply got the boat out on to the water with no effort, when Amy knew how much work he must have put into it to get it into shape again.

'Oh, thank you, Jim! I was hoping so much that she was ready for sea. I know what a mess she was in. Tell me how much and I'll pay you tonight.'

'You'll not, lass!' he said gruffly. ''Twere my fault in the first place, not getting her under cover before the storm broke last year.'

'I should have done it myself!' she protested, and he grinned at her sideways.

'And would have done, had it not been for Ralph keeping you talking until the last minute.'

Amy smiled as she remembered. His son Ralph had been rather too interested in her the last time she was here. That was one of the reasons that she had stayed away for so long.

'I expect he's going steady with some girl now?' she ventured hopefully; complications she did not need!

'No. Reckon he's still sweet on 'ee,' Jim said

laconically, reaching for her case. 'Come over and have some tea, lass. It's a long drive from London. I'll light the fire, or more than likely, Ralph will.'

'It's so good to be back here!' Amy sighed, stretching out in the big old armchair after an afternoon tea of scones with thick clotted cream and home-made strawberry jam, all washed down with strong, sweet tea. 'In a few days, I'll be as fat as butter!'

'Ay, we'll fatten you up!' Mrs Trehearne said with a pointed glance at Jim's waistline. ''Tis not difficult to do that.'

'Amy's like a greyhound, too much speed to put on weight, same as Ralph,' Jim said, making a point of his own.

Amy cringed inside. She knew how they cared about her and how they would have liked her to be back here in Port Garvith permanently. She didn't put a little matchmaking beyond their capabilities. She was really dreading the time when Ralph would come home.

'And where is Ralph?' she asked, taking the bull by the horns.

'Harbour,' said Jim with a sly grin, 'tending the pots. Would have sent to say that you'm here, but a surprise is good for anybody.'

Always providing that it's not a shock, Amy thought, her treacherous mind leading her back to Max and the woman at the theatre.

Ralph came in an hour later. By that time Amy had been back to her cottage and, while Jim had lit the fire in the small sitting-room, she had hauled out bedding to air and propped her mattress against one of the radiators that the fire provided hot water for—all innovations since her mother and father had lived so happily here.

She was back across the road, sitting talking to Mrs Trehearne, when Ralph came in, a big, fair-haired man with the look of the sea about his eyes and the beaten tan of the wind on his face.

'Amy!' He had to stoop to come in at the low door and he stopped in delighted surprise, his face reddening even further. 'I saw the car over the way and I hoped, but 'tis not the same one.'

He strode over and fairly yanked her to her feet, giving her a great hug before his natural shyness overcame him and he noticed the pleased and knowing grins on the faces of his parents and younger brother.

'I got a new car this year,' Amy told him when she had breathlessly extricated herself from this unexpected attack. 'Hello, Howie! You've grown again.'

'No, you've shrunk, I reckon!' Howard Trehearne was seventeen, a mirror image of his older brother, just left school and working with the older men for the first time as a paid hand.

She watched them all with a great fondness as they prepared for supper, talking all the time. In many ways they were still her people. They made their living on the wild and treacherous sea, and though Howie was only now a true fisherman, he had been on boats all his life, just as she would have done had she stayed here.

Her mind skimmed back to the little school overlooking the harbour, its low walls on the edge of the cliff. Each day, after school, many small boats put out to sea from there. They were small and inexpensive, manned by the children of the fishermen, who waited impatiently for the end of the school day to take their boats out on to the bright water. Howie had always done that, so had she, when she was not quite eight. It was their life. It had been hers, and she wondered if perhaps she would not have been happier staying in it. A strong, laughing face flashed into her mind, a face with silver-grey eyes, a man so strong that he could lift her effortlessly into the air. He called her many names from sweetheart to lunatic. He teased her, raged at her and made love to her until she trembled. No, whatever happened to her now, she would not have changed things. She would never regret Max.

They all talked until late, but they were up early. The lobster pots had to be tended, the keeping pots in the deep pools of the harbour checked as the tide stood at slack. Amy went down with Ralph and Howie, already dressed for the sea, her blue jeans topped by a thick sweater, white plimsolls on her feet and the bright yellow oilskin jacket that hung all the time behind the door in her cottage topping off her outfit.

Ralph helped her to get her bright blue dinghy into the water and then lifted his fair head to sniff the breeze.

'Rain before too long,' he said, with the certainty of years of knowledge. 'Better get her out within the next half-hour, Amy, or the wind will be off the sea and you'll never get through the gap.'

'Want to bet?' Amy asked, looking up into his smiling face.

'No, I wouldn't do that. You handle her well. Best to get into the Channel before the wind turns, though.'

Amy nodded and sighed happily.

'This is the life, Ralph! I just wish you'd tell Aunt Joan,

when next she's here, that I can handle a boat as well as a man.'

'Who said that?' laughed Ralph. 'I said you handle her well, for a snippet of a girl, that is.' He ducked as Amy aimed a friendly blow at him. 'Your aunt will always worry about you, anyway. May as well save your voice, she's a city woman.'

'So am I!' Amy said firmly, accepting his hand to help her into the boat, when she really needed no help at all.

'You're one of us, girl!' he insisted, sounding like his father, and adding with his mother's cunning, 'I bet your man worries about you, too.'

'Yes.' She automatically thought of Max. Nobody else was, or ever would be, her man. For a minute her eyes clouded, but she smiled up at Ralph as he stood on the harbour wall. 'He doesn't know I'm here, though. In fact, he doesn't know about this place at all, so I can do exactly as I like.'

She hadn't meant to use the conversation to warn Ralph off, but she suddenly realised that it probably had. He looked grim.

'Ralph,' she began worriedly, but he straightened up and looked at her with a wry smile.

'I suppose you'll stop coming down here before long, then?'

'I never will!' she rejoined heatedly. 'And anyway . . .'

'If you want him knocked down, I'm your man,' he said, hands on his hips, looking like a latter-day Viking, understanding her misery with no words actually said on the subject.

'Oh, Ralph, love,' she laughed, hoisting the clear red sail and making to move off. 'He's big, too, and strong as a bull. I wouldn't know who to back!'

'Maybe,' he said quietly, his eyes narrowed as *Bluebird* began to respond to the tiller and slid along on the water with the grace of its wondrous namesake.

It was exhilarating to be once more on the water. Amy felt the cold almost at once, and fastened her yellow oilskin, then began to manoeuvre the boat skilfully out of the harbour. Looking up, she could see the old school where she had started at five years old, so very different from the modern and rather impersonal place where she worked now. Grey, its woodwork white-painted, it looked like an old galleon perched there, its windows watching the Channel. On a stormy night, she had been told, you could hear the sea roar into the deep caves far below the cliff, the water sucking out again with a moaning that startled any new Headmaster who occupied the schoolhouse that was attached. His later anxious questioning would be a source of delight to the fishermen, until he fathomed it out for himself and met their dire tales with a grin that showed he had become part of the community.

The keeping pots were there, below the towering cliff that dropped to the harbour below the school, and Amy waved to Howie, who was already at work. Then she carefully steered through the breakwater and felt the tug of the wild water that waited beyond the harbour walls. The wind sang in her hair, and all fears and worries were forgotten. For a little while she was free of the pain of Max, free of all cares. She planted herself firmly and really began to sail as *Bluebird* headed out into the Bristol Channel and she challenged the sea as her father had done all his life, his father before him.

* * *

There was nothing to do but sail, take a drink with Ralph and Howie at the local pub and simply hang around the harbour, talking to the older fishermen who now did not go to battle with the sea. They talked of the men who had gone, of great storms and great catches and they spoke of her father, quietly, as if he were still there. It was what she needed, she always needed it. It anchored her irrepressible spirit, made her safe for a while.

She visited the coastguard station that stood on the point opposite the school, climbing the steep and twisting path instead of taking her car around the road. The cliffs fell away to the rocks that edged the sea, and she was thankful that Aunt Joan was not at the cottage, watching with her everlasting anxiety, the binoculars out to confirm her worst fears, that Amy had fallen.

It was from this old station that Amy had heard the bang of the maroons when she had lived here, a signal that had warned all the volunteers that someone was in danger, and in her carefree childhood it had been a great thrill to race out into the school yard, all lessons abandoned, to watch the in-shore rescue boat being launched, the Headmaster one of the volunteer crew. Nothing had changed, except herself. Unless she was sailing, out on the sea, she pined for Max. It was not going to go away.

'You're not the same,' Ralph said quietly one evening as they sat with drinks at the pub. Howie was playing darts and they were alone for the moment. 'A year ago, when you came home, you were a different girl.'

It rang a mournful bell in her mind. When she had gone back to Northumberland, Max had also said that she had gone home, but Max had said she was still the same old Amy, cheerful, cheeky and impetuous. She had changed during the course of the summer holiday. She had admitted love for Max. It was supposed to make you happy!

'You're in love with this man!' he added determinedly, when she said nothing. 'And he has someone else.'

'I was just as clever as you when we were at school, Ralph,' she said with a weak attempt to laugh it off. 'How have you got to be so smart now?'

'I stayed where I belonged. City living dulls the mind,' he said impatiently. 'So he doesn't love you?'

'He does, in his way,' Amy said softly. 'I suppose you might say that he's loved me all my life—well, since I was eleven. I used to think I knew him perfectly, every breath he took, but I didn't know him at all.'

'He left you?' Ralph looked furious, his voice almost a growl.

'No, he never belonged to me,' she admitted simply. 'I just wished it. I never did stop being childish.'

'I'd be down here after you, if it were me!' he said heatedly, his hand gripping his glass.

'He has no idea where I am. This is one secret I never told him, and now I never shall. Let's play darts. I can do as well as any of those!' She stood determinedly, ignoring the fierce and possessive anger on Ralph's face. How good it would have been if it had been Ralph she had loved, if she had stayed here and remained with her own people. The dark, smiling face came back into her mind, the tender, smiling eyes, and her own eyes blurred with tears. Max was 'her people'. Who was she trying to fool?

* * *

A whole week had passed and Amy was tanned and healthy, her skills on the water quite back to normal, her days taking on a soothing routine. Then Max arrived. She was in the garden, the small garden at the side of the cottage, that fought a losing battle yearly with the salt air of the wind. She never heard the car stop, and when he came round the corner she was crouching by the edge of the path, weeding. It was only his giant shadow, blocking the morning sunlight, that alerted her to the fact that she was not alone, and her face paled as she sprang to her feet.

'What are you doing here?' Her voice was startled, unfriendly and scared.

'You ran. Where else would I be but chasing after you?' He sounded utterly tired of her, and Amy crouched down again to gather the weeds, uncertain as to how she should act. There was none of the teasing in his voice, no smile in his eyes.

'I don't remember asking you to chase down here,' she assured him. 'In any case, I'm not running anywhere. I always come here for at least one week in the summer. I come here twice a year—the cottage is mine.'

'Thanks for telling me, after about eleven years!' he said tightly. 'As a matter of fact, I already know. Your aunt Joan told me.'

'She had no business!' Amy stood again and faced him, determinedly meeting his cool eyes.

'Do you think that you could offer me a drink and some breakfast?' he asked wearily. 'It's a hell of a drive down here. It was still dark when I set off.'

'I'm sorry, I never thought . . . You surprised me!' she

added angrily, and Max walked behind her to the door of the cottage.

'I surprise myself, almost daily!' he bit out in annoyance that was only partially directed at her.

Inside the cottage, which seemed to shrink as Max entered, she busily began to prepare breakfast, surprised to see that it was still only half-past eight. She had eaten ages ago, while Max was still driving down here.

'I'm not coming back with you!' She was furious with herself that she could not face him. He stood in the doorway of the small kitchen, watching her deft movements, and she was shaking like a leaf in a storm. She had absolutely no control over herself as far as Max was concerned, and it angered her; all her hard-won tranquillity had fled as her eyes had seen him.

'I don't recall asking you,' he murmured quietly.

'Then what are you doing here?' She spun round and faced him, her chin tilted aggressively.

'Following you.' He took the tray of tea from her hands and walked to the table that took up a great deal of the kitchen space. 'We eat here?'

'Yes! This isn't your stately mansion,' she said spitefully. 'This is mine. This is where I was born and where I lived. It's small and humble!'

'Unlike you,' murmured Max, quite loud enough for her to hear. 'You're merely small!'

'Now look here, Max——' she began, but his eyes were on the other room, the small and pretty sitting-room with its old dark beams and its brightly covered chairs.

'You did that?' he asked in surprise. 'You're a homemaker?' He took his tea and sauntered through.

'It's just as my mother left it,' Amy said quietly,

following him. 'It's been a long time but, as it's hardly ever used, the things have stayed fresh and bright.'

'You don't let it?' he enquired, wandering around.

'No. It's mine, my home!' She was very agitated, on the edge of tears, everything made worse when Max stopped to look at the photograph of her mother and father, and then at one taken on the harbour wall, her father sitting with Amy on his knee; two dark heads close together, two pairs of blue eyes smiling into the camera, Amy as tiny as a doll.

'I remember you,' Max said softly, adding as she stood silently, 'Your father?'

'Yes.' Amy swallowed hard and lifted the framed photograph. 'He was a fisherman—the best! We had a boat that took four hands besides my father. We weren't rich, but we weren't poor, either. Then, one day, he took my mother with him as a treat. It was her birthday. I stayed with Mrs Trehearne. Her husband was having the day off to make room for my mother. They never came back. *Prudence* went down with all hands.'

'That's what it was called, *Prudence*?'

'Yes, my mother's name. He loved her very much.'

Max turned and looked at her, the weariness still on his face.

'Don't you think that it's time to let them go, Amy?' he asked softly.

'The bacon's burning.' Once again she fled, and he did not follow.

'I noticed there are no windows on the seaward side of the house,' Max observed as he ate the breakfast Amy had cooked, while she sat at the table, drinking tea. He had made no further reference to her parents or to the fact that he had come down here to her.

'No, I don't know about now, but in the past it wasn't allowed. Any lights could attract ships, could be mistaken for the lights used to guide them, and the coast is so dangerous.'

'Wreckers,' Max said knowingly.

'Not everybody,' Amy said, getting herself a slow and considering look. She hadn't been making a point, but he seemed to think so.

'Well, I'm going to sail now.' Amy sprang up and cleared the dishes into the sink. 'These can wait.'

'Is that what I'm supposed to do?' Max asked in sudden anger. 'Would you like me to sit beside the dishes until you have a minute?'

'Look, I didn't ask you to come here. I have my day planned. My boat will be out on the water now, Jim will have got it out.' She snatched up her oilskin jacket and made for the door, Max right behind her.

'And who the hell is Jim?' he asked aggressively, grabbing her arm.

'An old friend of my father,' she snapped. What right did he have to even ask? Had she demanded to know who the beautiful woman was when she had seen him at the theatre?

'Everything all right, Amy?' Ralph and Howie were just coming out of their cottage, and Ralph's face was menacing, his expression quite similar, actually, to the one on Max's face.

'Perfectly. I'm taking *Bluebird* out as usual.'

'We'll go down together, then,' Ralph said determinedly, and she was only too happy to agree. Any moment now, and she would be throwing herself into

Max's arms, asking why he didn't want her after all.

'Aren't you going to lock the door?' Max asked in a low and angry voice, his eyes on the tall, fair-haired fisherman who seemed to be very possessive about Amy.

She never got the chance to answer; Ralph and Howie did that for her.

'Lock the door?' scoffed Howie, his face a mixture of surprise and annoyance.

'Amy is among her own kind!' Ralph said shortly. 'Nobody can hurt her here.'

It was not the kind of atmosphere for introductions, and Amy never tried. She felt the need to walk beside Max—not that he looked or ever had looked as if he needed protection, but more because she felt that the two armed camps should be separated. And, horribly, nobody spoke. She felt like Gulliver among the giants, every one of them angry.

At the harbour, the two brothers left her and got out their skiff, ready to check over the pots, but there were others there, old fishermen who called out to her, using her first name. Max said nothing until she was right beside her boat.

'I'm coming with you!'

He glared down at her and she stepped quickly into *Bluebird*, casting off and gliding just out of reach.

'It's a one-man boat. It wouldn't balance with two.'

'These are dangerous waters, your aunt Joan said so. I want to come with you, Amy.'

'I don't need you! I can handle any boat, and this is my own. I can handle anything and anybody!'

Amy just drifted away and then began to make her way across the harbour, ignoring his angry and frustrated voice. She had to get out on the water. She was torn between the two worlds that she loved, but Max was here, Max was calling, and if she didn't hurry, she would just simply give in. And she didn't even know what he wanted any more. She turned *Bluebird* to the harbour entrance and slid through with a competent and graceful ease, turning head-on into the wind and out into the Channel, feeling that she had pulled away from Max by sheer willpower, wanting to run back to him as she had always done.

CHAPTER NINE

IT was wonderfully pure out on the rocking water.
Nothing clouded the mind. High, scudding clouds that
raced along, seeming to keep pace with the flashing
movement of the bright blue boat and the gentle swell,
gave a perfect atmosphere for tranquillity. Amy sat in the
stern, handling the dancing boat almost automatically,
her mind racing with the clouds, working out the
problems that seemed to be upon her so suddenly.

Max had come down here, and he had called it 'chasing
after her'. He had said he had simply followed her, not
demanding that she return, and that was different. When
he had seen her in London and suspected her of having a
man in the house, his attitude had been one of protection.
What was his attitude now? Did he simply want to be with
her? And what about the beautiful woman at the theatre?

She could go on thinking this over for the rest of her life,
until there was no life left. He had asked her to give up the
past, her ties here, and she realised she had clung to them,
mentally if not physically. Why would she be giving them
up? For Max? She suddenly remembered his face when he
had come, weary and with a total acceptance of his role, to
follow when she ran.

She moved swiftly, putting about on the sparkling
water, heading for the harbour that was still in sight. She
had never been without courage, had never held her
tongue when something needed to be said. She had to
know how Max felt, and for some reason he was not going

to tell her. Dreading the worst was a much more horrific thing than finding it out.

Her chin set firmly and her eyes narrowed against the sun. She would tackle him head-on, and if he laughed at her she would tell him to go and stay out of her life. It was all or nothing from now on! She couldn't live like this.

Amy was almost at the harbour mouth when the dull thud of the maroon echoed across the water, and her eyes were instantly alert. There were no other boats out, only her own *Bluebird*. The sea was calm except for the turbulence around the rocks at the base of the cliffs. Every year, holidaymakers landed themselves in trouble, doing foolish things that put their lives at risk, and she knew it was even worse in the bigger places where holidaymakers gathered in larger numbers. They had their share here, though, in Port Garvith. It often appeared that when people packed their bags for the holiday, they left their common sense behind at home. The cliffs, that seemed to be so easy to descend, usually proved to be impossible to climb without help, and often the inshore rescue boat was launched to pick people off the rocks before the tide got them.

And so it was now. Amy saw the child as she scanned the cliff face opposite the school. He was no more than six or seven, clinging to the rocks outside the harbour entrance, a dangerous and turbulent place, where the calm harbour waters met the heavy swell of the Bristol Channel. What lunatic had allowed this? No local child would have placed himself in such danger. His parents were probably sitting in the sun, quite sure that all would be well, merely because they were at the seaside.

Glancing at the boathouse, she could see the rescue boat being dragged out to the slipway, a bright orange inflatable boat that could skim in close to the rocks. She could also see the child, foolishly trying to move, forsaking his safe ledge in a futile attempt to climb to safety. He would be in the water long before the boat got here.

She put *Bluebird* hard over, turning her head to the cliffs, the wind steady behind her.

'Keep still!' Her clear voice rang across the water, carrying like a bell on the morning air.

"Tis Amy!' Ralph Trehearne straightened for a second as he helped with the rescue boat, and it even stopped the others in their tracks. 'She's seen him, she's taking *Bluebird* in!'

'She'll smash into the rocks! Amy!' There was such a desolation in the cry of the stranger with grey eyes who had come this morning, that Jim Trehearne put his hand on the man's arm.

'She knows the place as well as we do. She can handle that boat like a born sailor.' It was a kindhearted attempt to ease away worry, but it had little effect; the tall, powerful man was stiff with anxiety, not speaking, and they could see her clearly now—the bright blue boat flying towards the cliffs, Amy's yellow jacket brilliantly clear against the red sail. She still had the sails up, the mainsail and jib filled with the wind from the Channel, carrying the boat in like a racing horse.

'Amy!' Max's voice was hoarse with pain as he watched, mesmerised by the sight of her, then he dived forward as the rescue boat was launched, the crew almost tumbling into it.

'Stay here! She'll come about, 'tis not a suicide attempt!' Jim said sharply, grabbing him.

'The only way to get in there.' The other old fishermen came to Jim's aid, voicing their opinions, watching Amy without any apparent worry, their eyes flicking from the orange boat that raced across the harbour to the flashing blue dinghy that was heading straight for the rocks.

It was a question of gauging the moment. She could see the child clearly now, and he was terrified, his position much more precarious than it had been at first. If only he would keep his nerve. If she could keep hers! The rocks were close, but she knew that they shelved straight down. It could be done.

At the last minute she came about, ducking the boom, acting speedily as she dropped the mainsail, praying that she had judged the time right. She went in on her forward impetus, the boat now sideways to the rocks, going in on the lap of the waves, two yards, one, and then only a couple of feet. She dropped everything and stood on the dangerously rocking boat, her foot fending off the rocks as she reached for the boy—and he jumped!

It seemed for a moment that everything would be all right; the boat rocked wildly, leaping away from the sharp-edged rocks and then righting itself. But the cliff seemed to be on top of them, and before she could act further the child lunged for her, clinging to her for safety and comfort, and *Bluebird* went over, both of them with it.

Amy's only thought was of the child and how pointless it had all been. She surfaced by the boat, reaching out and grabbing him as he, too, came to the surface.

'Hold on hard!' she shouted at him to bring him to his senses, and he nodded, his small hands gripping the upturned dinghy as Amy clung beside him, her arm across his back to take some of the weight.

The oilskin jacket was dragging her down, heavy, its pockets and the hood filled with water, and she began to shrug out of it.

'Hang on while I get rid of this!' Her gyrations took his attention from his own predicament, and he clung more tightly until she was free of the jacket and holding him again, four hands instead of two clinging to the boat, Amy's body behind him, anchoring him fast.

Dazedly, she followed his rapt gaze. The yellow oilskin jacket drifted away, bright upon the water, its arms outstretched, its skirt spread out as if she were still in there. She might have been. The child shuddered and she gave him a warm kiss on his cheek.

'Here comes the rescue boat,' she said, with more heartiness than she felt, and he glanced at her sideways, tears on his cheeks.

'I wrecked your boat, lady. My dad will be so mad!'

'Nonsense!' Amy's arm tightened round him as the boat pulled alongside. She had never been called 'lady' before, it had an odd ring. She was wet and cold, but no longer unhappy. Max was at the cottage, and she would run towards him this time.

'That was some going, Amy!' Howie helped to haul her in as Ralph took the child. 'A beautiful sight to see.'

'He jumped!' said Amy, with a rueful look at the small boy, who was being wrapped in a thick blanket.

'We saw!' Ralph said laconically, glancing at her. 'Your man's going out of his mind. Reckon he's not used to the sea.'

'Max? Max saw all that?' She suddenly realised what it must have looked like to him. He might have lived by the coast all his life, but he was not of the sea as these men were. They would have read her every action, Max would only have seen the worst. She turned her head, frantically trying to see him as they crossed the harbour, astonished to find that her love also contained a protective instinct. Was this how he felt when she ran?

He was still there as they cut the motor and cruised up to the steps, and his face was completely white, his eyes intent on Amy's face as she sat on the boat with a blanket over her.

'Well done, lass!' There were cries from all the men gathered there, and she could see that Ralph's eyes were hard as he looked among the small crowd for the parents who had left their child to such risk.

'We'll get *Bluebird*. Not to worry, Amy.' Howie's voice was reassuring as he helped her to dry land. 'I reckon she'll be no worse than she was after the storm.'

'Thanks, Howie.' Amy stood a little forlornly, her eyes on Max. So far, he had made no move towards her and she knew he was blaming her for the fright he had suffered. She was once again classed as madcap, a lunatic, idiotic. For a second, their eyes held, and then he moved, clasping her to him, wrapping the blanket tightly around her and holding her so close that she could hardly breathe.

'Amy, why did you do that? Why didn't you leave that child for the rescue boat?'

"'Tis the currents.' Jim Trehearne strolled up, interrupting the scene with no qualms. 'If the boy had stayed still, he would have been all right. He wasn't going to, though, and Amy saw. If he'd slipped then, he would have been taken round the corner, more than likely, and he would've been gone before the men got there. 'Tis a wicked undertow.'

'And what about you, Amy? Suppose you'd gone round the corner?' demanded Max in a hoarse voice.

'Amy's one of us!' Ralph Tremaine said tightly. 'She knows, same as we do!'

'Jim, *Bluebird*'s wrecked!' Amy said shakily, not able to

face Ralph's antagonism to Max, or anything else for that matter.

'I'll fix her!' Jim grinned at her and glanced at Max. 'Didn't I tell 'ee? There's no need to fuss about Amy. Morgan Tremaine were the best, and she's still his girl.'

Max turned her away abruptly, his arm tightly around her as he walked up the steep hill to the cottage without another word. Amy was shivering, although she was not in the least cold. Her jeans were stiffly wet, rubbing uncomfortably against her legs, and it was even more difficult to walk with his arm around her, but she would not have protested for anything in the world.

Inside the cottage, he shut the door with a bang, his shoulders rising and falling just once, as he sighed deeply, like a man who had won against all odds.

'Better get out of those wet things,' he said gruffly. 'I'll find my own way around the kitchen and make you a hot drink when you've showered.' He turned away from her and walked into the small kitchen, and after a second of tearfully looking at his back, Amy went upstairs to the shower.

She had spoiled it all again. Max would never understand. If he had been in her place, he would have done the same thing; any of the men would, and it would have been fine if the boy had waited for her to reach for him instead of jumping. As it was, all Max had seen was danger for her, and he had so clearly thought it was her attitude to life—action without thought, good old Amy! She would be classed as an idiot child for ever.

She dropped the blanket on the floor and went into the shower, discarding her wet clothes as she stepped under the hot spray. Inside, she was angry and frustrated, love mixed up with annoyance. Max had left her with the uncomfortable feeling that she had been merely showing off. He had never thought to say 'Well done,' as the others had. She had not risked everything for praise, only to save the boy, but to hear a small amount of praise from Max for her actions, for her common sense, would have been heavenly. He praised her beauty, building a small shrine to it, he praised the way she moved, capturing it in bronze, but to him she was still a wild and impetuous child.

She wrapped herself in a towel and padded to her room, still muttering to herself as she used the drier on her short, crisp hair, almost beating it off her head with the brush in her annoyance, the brush still in her hand, like a weapon, when Max simply walked in.

'Why can't you knock like anybody else would?' stormed Amy as she saw him. 'I'm quite capable of coming down for my cup of tea or whatever it is!'

He put the offending cup on her dressing-table and said nothing, even when she stormed on.

'I'm sick of you treating me like a stupid child! I'm sick of you chasing all over after me to see that I don't get into scrapes! I do *not* get into scrapes! I'm a fully grown woman with responsibilities, and I would have still been here, wet, safe and tired, even if you'd stayed in London or wherever you were!'

Max stared at her for a second, his face curiously stiff, his eyes almost dark with some emotion.

'You're so small,' he said in a voice that seemed to hurt him. 'I suppose I've never really quite understood that you're extremely capable physically, that your athletic skills are not some kind of a magical trick. I wonder if every man feels as I do about some woman? You were racing to the cliffs, doing something I can't do, in spite of my strength. I wanted to pick you out of danger, get to

you, and God, I tried! Those three old imbeciles wouldn't
let me go! That bloody Jim of yours had an arm lock
round my neck, and his damned cronies pounced on me
like a pack of escaped lunatics. I had to stand there while
you raced to what I thought would be your death, and all
the time they were simply praising you! "Look at the lass
go!" "She'll come about now!" Do you know that while I
was going out of my mind there was a chap there taking
photographs with a camera with a great lens like a
telescope? You'll no doubt be in the papers again,
"Former medal winner in rescue dash!" I don't want you
to win any medals. I want you safe in my hands, in my
arms—you're my woman!'

For a second Amy just stared at him, her eyes wide and
astonished at such raw emotion, the pained words that she
had never thought Max capable of still ringing in her ears.
Then she ran and threw her arms around him, hugging
him to her, wanting for once to be big and powerful like
him so that she could rock him in her arms as he now
rocked her.

'Are you going to beat me with that brush?' he said
unsteadily, and she let it drop to the floor.

'Oh no, Max! I'm going to love you and love you!'

'I deserve it,' he said, kissing her cheeks urgently, 'but
right now I'm not capable of standing it.'

'I'm so sorry I frightened you, Max,' she whispered.
'There was nothing else I could do. I had no idea you were
still there. If the boy had let me take him, instead of
jumping into *Bluebird*, I could have brought him in myself,
and then you wouldn't have been so upset.'

'I saw your yellow jacket,' he said huskily. 'It was
floating on the water. I thought you were still in it,
drowning. That's when I tried to jump in and get you—

the boat had gone under by then.'

'You were going to swim out there?' Amy stepped back and looked at him with panic in her eyes. 'Max, it was in the current as it floated away! You would have been the one to drown!'

'They wouldn't let me!' he rasped, still angered by her friends. 'When I looked like getting away, that Jim person called up reinforcements!'

'Oh, thank God for Jim!' Amy said fervently. She hung on to him even tighter. 'I'll never come to Cornwall again. I'll sell the cottage, then you'll never be here. I'll let Port Garvith out of my life for ever!'

'But you're Morgan Tremaine's girl,' Max reminded her softly, tilting her flushed face and looking intently into her brilliantly blue eyes.

'No,' she whispered, her feelings so very clear to see. 'I'm your girl. I have been for years, and I knew it. I've only just admitted it to myself.'

'So what do you want to be to me, Amy?' he asked quietly, his arms tightly around her.

'Everything,' she said softly. 'Whatever you want me to be.'

'You're small, beautiful, graceful and filled with the most astonishing talents,' he murmured, looking down at her. 'When you're out of my sight, I'm in a panic because you have this ability to find trouble and race right into it.' His lips brushed hers lightly before he looked at her again. 'You know what I want you to be, that's why you run. That's why you've run since you were seventeen. I want to own every exquisite part of you. You're my woman, and wherever you go, I'll be one step behind you.'

'I'm not going anywhere,' she whispered shakily, her

legs beginning to tremble as his hands caressed her bare shoulders.

'Not right now, you're not,' he said quietly. 'Unless you're not up to it after your wild rescue bid.'

'W-would you listen if I said I was very shaken?' Amy asked tremulously, gasping when his fingers slid into the top of the towel and stroked the swollen rise of her breast.

'No,' he murmured against her ear. 'I came down here to get you. It's been difficult to lay hands on you, but I've got you now. Unless you want to start a fight?'

'I'm too tired to fight,' she admitted with a shaken smile, clinging to him when he suddenly lifted her into his arms. 'I'll fight later.'

'You won't want to, my darling,' he promised, laying her on the bed and leaning over her. 'You said you were going to love me and love me. That's what I'm going to do to you, but I'll let you join in.'

He watched her, seeing the flash of uneasiness that clouded her face for a second, then the grey eyes were smiling again.

'Oh, my sweet, crazy, adorable Amy,' he said softly, 'you know that if you don't want me, I'll never touch you.'

'But I *do*, I do want you!' she said seriously. 'It's just that—that you're who you are. There's such a lot between us, so many years of knowing each other.'

'I can't pretend not to know you, although there are so many things about you that I don't know.' Max's hand stroked her face gently. 'I want to find out the things I don't know. I want to discover all of them while you're in my arms.'

'Max!' It was a small cry of longing and her arms came up, soft and clinging, to wind around his neck as she pulled him down to her, and he needed no second bidding. She was wrapped in his arms, wrapped in his strength at once, her breath escaping in a long sigh of happiness as he kissed her eyes, her cheeks, the velvet smoothness of her neck.

He seemed to be content to simply hold her and trail kisses over her skin, slowly and languorously, until her eyes closed and she lay quietly in his arms, her fingers stroking his hair. The heavy peace began to leave her as his lips searched for her, softly and gently at first, catching her mouth in short, tasting kisses that it seemed would never stop, teasing and playful, winding her up inside until she grasped his head and fused her lips with his own.

Then he drew her fully into his arms, crushing her against him, parting her lips to kiss her with a deep, searching intensity that sent waves of heat through her. And she was back on the beach in the moonlight, back in the house with the storm raging outside. Her hands clutched his shoulders as she softened to the hard power of his body.

'Max! Max!' her little cries escaped as he lifted his head to look at her, and he pulled his sweater over his head, casting it aside in one smooth movement, and unwinding the towel that hid her from him.

'In my mind, I already know you,' he said huskily, his eyes roaming hungrily over her. 'There's not one part of you that I haven't imagined. I've wanted you for so long, wanted you so very much, that it's been little short of madness.'

There was such a vibrant passion in his voice, such a pent-up desire that Amy closed her eyes again, tremblingly aware of his eyes on her, his hands on her skin. His voice was telling her he had wanted her for so long and her mind remembered the gentle, teasing man who had shown only care for her. His passion had been inside, his desire hidden, but there was no mistaking it now.

His lips began to trail over her skin, following the track of his hands, as he fashioned her body as if he were indeed creating her, his obsession. There was no time, though, to be afraid of this obsession, her mind spun away from all other thoughts. She was here with Max, locked in his arms, and the glorious wonder of it swept through her like a forest fire as her own hands reached for him, running over the strength of his back, the smooth power of his chest.

'You're so slight, so petite, I'm afraid to hurt you,' he muttered on a breath of desperation, as she moved compulsively against the hard potency of his body.

'I'm not weak! I'm terribly strong,' she gasped, twisting in a desperation of her own as his hands caressed her.

'When I see you move, you seem to be a match for me at any time. You're sparky and quick-tempered and I know you're so full of life. When I hold you, though, like this, you're delicate, dainty, almost untouchable.'

She wound her arms around him and something seemed to snap inside him. His tender caresses became sensual and demanding, his lips hotly pressed to her skin, his body urgently against hers.

'No going back, Amy, for either of us,' he murmured against the sharp peak of her breast. 'Now you're mine! I'm not going to let you dance free, my little nymph.'

Amy had no desire to dance free, she wanted to be part of Max, and her soft moaning told him so as he moulded her to him, whispering softly and encouragingly against her skin, urging her into a frenzy of desire that exploded into pain and delight at the sudden and powerful thrust of his body.

She was too aroused to feel more than a brief flare of

pain, and it seemed to her dazzled mind that Max discounted it, he was too committed to owning her body and soul, the tender, gentle, smiling Max gone as he looked at her with blazing eyes and took her with him into another world.

Amy came out of the velvet darkness and warmth of it to open her eyes and see him watching her, a hunger still flaring in the depths of his silvery gaze. He never spoke, never moved, and her flushed cheeks grew rosy at the possessive look of him.

'You hurt me!' she pouted, her blue eyes sliding away in shyness, and his fingers stroked her face, then smoothed her tumbled hair from her forehead.

'You're too dainty to make love to,' he assured her teasingly, his voice curiously thick and low. 'Maybe it should never happen again.' His eyes flashed with a silver fire as she turned swiftly with a look of sheer fright on her face, and waves of heat flooded through her as he tightened her in his arms.

'Don't tease me like that!' she begged softly, and Max smiled a slow and secret smile.

'But darling, I have to! It's the only way I can live with it. If I behaved in any way normally, I'd be devouring you all the time, and then where would we be?'

'Here!' Amy sighed, arching against him as his lips claimed her with an urgent passion.

They went down to the harbour later to see if *Bluebird* had been salvaged, and Max grunted irritably as he spotted Jim Trehearne with his cronies, all standing around Amy's boat.

'Hardly damaged at all, Amy!' called Jim, his sharp eyes taking in Amy's happy face and the tight, possessive hand that held hers. 'She's not holed at all. I'll give her a rinse out and set her right, then mend the jib. Nothing else is wrong. You can take her out again tomorrow.'

'No,' Amy said quietly. 'I'll not be taking her out again.'

'Amy?' Max looked down at her in surprise. 'You love the boat, that's clear. You're a fine sailor—these old lunatics said so,' he added in a low murmur.

'There are more things in my life than the sea,' Amy said softly, looking at him with brilliantly alive blue eyes. 'When she's finished, Jim,' she said, turning to the man who watched her with astonishment, 'I want you to give her to one of the children, one who can handle her and enjoy her.'

He opened his mouth to protest, but she sidetracked him quickly. 'Did that little boy get to his parents safely?'

'Ay, Ralph found them.' He looked a little rueful. 'He can be hard at times, can Ralph. They'll not be letting that happen again!'

'I won't let you give up this place,' Max said steadily as they walked through the village. 'I won't let you sell the cottage, either. You don't have to give up the things you love for me, Amy.'

'Then we'll come here and explore Cornwall,' she said happily, her eyes alight. 'I'll show you every square inch of it!'

'By land!' Max put in determinedly, his arm coming round her.

They stood watching the sea, watching the men bending over the nets, and Amy shivered with happiness and remembered pleasure. She pushed from her mind the fact that she still did not know what she was to Max, besides an obsession; she refused to think of the woman at the theatre, the beautiful, polished grace of her. For now

Max was hers, and she clung to his hand as he looked down into her eyes with a sensuous, narrowed gaze.

'Good grief!' Amy sniffed the air. Somebody was cooking, and the delicious smell drifted on the breeze. 'I never had lunch!'

'Neither did I!' laughed Max, 'but then, I'm not a voracious carnivore. Want to go out for a meal?'

'No! I've got at least two days' food in the cottage. I'm going to cook you a really splendid meal!'

'Right, you can cook the lot, then, because tomorrow we're going home,' Max said determinedly. 'Tonight we'll have a huge, early dinner and then we'll have an early night. We'll leave in the morning, before anyone here can persuade you to stay!'

'If you tried to leave without me, I'd follow you!' Amy said with a swift look at him.

'That really would make a nice change,' Max remarked with a wry smile as he turned her towards the cottage.

It was wonderful, cooking for Max, and she was a good cook. She shooed him out of the kitchen and got started at once, peering in at him later to see that he was reading in the small, bright sitting-room. It made her start to dream, but she stifled the dreams at once. For now, she had Max and she was happy. The future would take care of itself.

'That was good!' Max said later when they sat back, replete. 'I never thought you could cook.'

'You underestimate me all the time!' Amy told him with a laugh. 'I'll surprise you yet!'

'You've surprised me enough for one day,' he said softly, his eyes skimming over her. 'Let's wash these dishes and then I'll take you for a drink at that little pub by the harbour. I want everyone to see that you're happy with me, and that I'm not kidnapping you.' He looked at her sideways, his glance keen. 'I think you should let Ralph down gently.'

'I can't help it—about Ralph, I mean. I've never encouraged him. I . . .'

'You don't have to, sweetheart. You only have to be there. I should know!' He pointed her in the direction of the kitchen and she went, but she did think about that woman and how *she* had looked. Maybe Max was allowed to be jealous and she wasn't? It somehow fitted into the unfair scheme of things!

CHAPTER TEN

THEY started for home early the next day. Amy had expected to drive behind Max, but he would not hear of it.

'There's no way I'll let you out of my sight,' he had said determinedly. 'I'll get someone to collect your car when we get back. There are services that exist for such times, and meanwhile, I'm quite sure it will be safe. If anyone so much as looked at your possessions, I'm certain the whole village would turn to and attack them. I feel quite relieved to have escaped with my life!'

Amy sat beside him, smiling. She was happy beyond her wildest dreams. She had no idea of her position in Max's life. She supposed rather dreamily that she was his mistress. It had a dramatic and startling ring to it. He had simply said that they were going home, and she imagined that she would be expected to explain it all to her aunt. But for now she cared for nothing.

The sun shone, the car went smoothly and quietly, and Max was back to being the Max she had known all her life, his powerful hands on the wheel, his face softened by the night they had spent together.

Amy was happy, too, about the previous evening that they had spent with her friends. Their arrival in the small, low-ceilinged pub, which had probably once been the haunt of smugglers, had stopped all conversation at first. Jim was there with Ralph and Howie, and for a few minutes she had thought that there would be trouble.

Ralph's face was like thunder. Then Jim had broken the ice by laughing openly at Max and buying him a drink, going over the morning's events for the benefit of his cronies and the other customers. Max had taken the ragging with a great grin that endeared him to the older men at once.

'In my opinion,' Jim had said finally, 'he thought Amy was dead set on self-destruction, tearing at the cliff to smash *Bluebird* up. Reckon it must have been a great quarrel they had to put such an idea into his head!'

'I've been watching her throw herself into danger for most of her life,' Max had explained, his arm coming around her. 'Nothing surprises me, but she can still frighten the life out of me.'

He'd ended up playing darts with them, and Amy had been sitting alone when Ralph had come away from the dartboard to sit beside her.

'So that's your man, after all, Amy girl?'

'I surely hope so, Ralph!' she'd said, with a rueful smile that explained her distress at his own feelings. Her hand had covered his. 'I suppose I've loved him all my life, more or less.'

'Well,' he'd ventured, swallowing hard and squeezing her hand, 'he's about as crazy for you as anyone can get.'

'Oh, Ralph, I hope so!' she'd breathed, her eyes on Max's laughing face as he talked to Jim. 'I don't know what I'd do if he didn't love me.'

'Reckon you're as daft as he seems to think, after all,' Ralph had snorted. 'If he turned round now and you weren't right here, he'd be going mad in seconds.'

Amy turned her head and looked at Max in the morning sunlight. Did he really love her as she loved him?

How long would this thing between them last?

'I hope to God you're not making any of your odd plans!' Max said without even glancing at her, his lips curved into a wry smile.

'I was thinking, that's all,' she said quietly.

'So tell me!' he demanded.

'I was wondering how long this would last,' she said, with her usual forthright honesty. 'I was thinking about the future and how I'll feel if you decide to . . .' Suddenly her voice broke, taking her completely by surprise, and she felt the unexpected burn of tears behind her eyes. 'Damn!'

'Didn't I tell you that you carry your own drama about with you?' he said, pulling her to his shoulder and keeping his arm around her.

'I think this is against the law,' she sniffed as he held her there and drove with one hand.

'Then you watch for the law and I'll just enjoy holding you,' he said comfortably. 'I can't promise to hold you until we get to Northumberland, but, if things get too bad, we'll stop for the night. That seems to have a good effect on you!'

'Northumberland? Max, I can't go back up there! I thought, when you said home, that you meant London. Max—I have to start school in about a week!'

'We'll see,' he murmured with infuriating calm.

'What do you mean, "we'll see"? I have to be there when the new term begins.'

'And if you're not?' he asked quietly.

'I—I don't know. I rather think I'd be in some sort of trouble!'

'Which wouldn't matter a damn, if you never went back at all!'

'That's called breaking your contract!'

'Well,' he drawled, 'I rather think that's what you're going to do, my darling. I work in Northumberland, my studio is there. Imagine the difficulties. A drive down to London every night for bedtime—it would wear me out!'

Amy sighed deeply in exasperation. 'Max, please be serious for a while!'

'I *am* serious,' he said quietly. 'I cannot and will not let you go again. Wherever we live, Amy, you and I live together, eat together and sleep together. I earn more than you do and I therefore demand the right to continue with my work. One of us must stop, and I've decided it will be you!'

'Male chauvinist pig!' Amy exclaimed wildly, pulling to a sitting position and removing his arm with a certain amount of violence. 'I can't stand your attitude!'

'Right, I'll drop you in London and continue alone!'

She was silent for a while, stunned by this turn of events. Max expected her to give everything up simply to live with him, and he was taking her to Northumberland, to Belmore House! Did he intend that they should live together there? She bit her lip and glanced sideways at him, but she could tell nothing from his expression.

'Max?' She spoke softly and worriedly, and he raised one dark, enquiring eyebrow.

'Darling?'

'I don't know what to do!' She looked at him woefully and he grinned to himself, holding out his arm for her, kissing her hair when she came to him with a rush and snuggled against him.

'I know—you need to make a decision. I've already made mine. It's equality for all, sweet Amy. You make yours now.'

'You've left me no choice,' she muttered crossly.

'Of course I have! Stay with me or go to that wretched school and bounce about the gym.'

'You know I can't leave you!' she said pitifully, and he pulled into the side of the road, taking her into his arms and capturing her startled mouth with his.

'That's what I banked on, my own Amy,' he murmured. 'Now that we know where we stand, we'll get along home.'

He simply pulled off after sitting her upright, her lips stinging with the passion of his kiss, her legs trembling, and after a minute, she began to laugh softly.

'That's my girl,' he said with a smile, and she sighed contentedly. How right he was; there was no other place that she could be but with Max.

She simply let him drive northwards with no further protests, allowing her mind to disregard the worries that threatened to cloud it. When they arrived there would be problems. Everyone would want to know what was happening. Her aunt Joan would have to be contacted, her school. She was throwing her whole life away without a qualm, just because Max wanted her, but she could never simply let him go. When he left her it would be his decision.

They had started early, before the small fishing village was awake, but the distance was great and, with stops for lunch and afternoon tea, it was after six in the evening before they reached Northumberland. Of course, it was still light and the sunny and warm weather had miraculously continued.

Amy raised her head from its safe resting place against Max's shoulder and almost sniffed the air.

'Home?' he asked quietly, and she smiled, though a little ruefully.

'I think it is,' she confessed. 'Jim wouldn't like to hear me say it, but this place has been home to me for more years than I can remember.'

'They're very fond of you down there,' Max assured her, although she already knew that. 'There's really no reason why you shouldn't go there frequently. It will make them all happy, including you.'

'What about you?' Amy asked softly, longing for him to give her the answer she needed. And of course, he did.

'Naturally I'll go with you, our separation being impossible for reasons I've just stated.'

'I wanted you to say that,' she whispered, kissing his cheek. 'You seemed to get on well enough with Jim, and I've made my peace with Ralph. What were you talking about to Jim, by the way?' she added inquisitively.

'Ah,' Max smiled secretly. 'I could tell you not to ask, but I know you well enough to realise that if I did that, you'd never let the matter drop. I was giving him a small but necessary order. I instructed him to repair *Bluebird* and keep it for you.'

'What? But Max, you know you'll hate it if I decide to sail again!'

'I know you'll miss it if you give it up,' he countered. 'It's in the blood, or so Jim assured me. I wouldn't want you any different.'

'I love you, Max,' she said very softly, and he smiled without looking at her.

'Do you, baby?' he asked quietly. 'I've been rather banking on it.'

They did not drive to Belmore House straight away. Max turned off before they got there, and Amy sat up straight as she realised just where they were going.

'We're going to see your house?' she asked breathlessly.

'Yes.' He did not correct her when she called it his house, and a small cloud crossed her mind. 'I want you to see the latest innovations. It's still light, and there's plenty of time to get to Belmore House. As they don't even know we're coming, they'll have no worries when we don't arrive until later.'

It had been really worked on, Amy could see that, and the garden had been actually finished. Max must have had an army of workmen here to get things to the stage that they had reached.

'Come inside and see the stairs,' he suggested, taking her arm. 'No more sprained ankles!'

It had been completely altered, the whole of the flight of stairs removed and a brand new copy of it installed. Hardly breathing, Amy walked into the lounge—and stopped suddenly.

'Well, what do you think of your ideas now they're visible to the naked eye?' Max asked drily, coming in behind her.

'I'm much cleverer than I ever imagined,' she retorted, her eyes moving over the room that she had visualised when she had come here. He had done everything she had suggested, every colour was her idea.

'Anything I've done wrong can be altered,' he said evenly. 'Only one more room to see—you never made any comments about the others, so I hardly dared to even look in them, in case I got ideas of my own.'

He led her up the stairs and into the bedroom he had called his. It was finished, creams and pinks predominating, with a deep pink carpet.

'You—you said they'd get funny ideas about you if you ordered a pink carpet,' muttered Amy, her face almost frozen with a sudden fear.

'Women like things like this, though,' Max commented softly, coming behind her and winding his arms around her, pulling her back to him. 'This is where we'll live, Amy, in this house. We'll sleep in this room. I know you like it. I knew you liked it the very first time you saw it.'

'I can't!' She pulled away and went to look out of the window. 'I can't live here in this house with you, Max.'

'Because you thought I was buying it for Glenys?' he asked in a puzzled voice. 'Darling, you know now, surely, that it was for you?'

'I—I can't live so close to Belmore House,' she whispered. 'It—it's almost within walking distance!'

'But, Amy, I thought you'd want to be close to the family. You're so full of life, my sweetest girl, I never want to keep you locked away from the people and the things you love.'

'I do, I did want to be near them, but—but Max, I can't just live with you *here*! What would they think? What would they say?'

He walked to her and turned her, his hands on her shoulders.

'Wait a minute! You plan to simply live with me? You wicked child! I can see I'm going to have to teach you a few old-fashioned virtues. You'll marry me, miss, or I'll put you over my knee and spank you until you do!'

Amy just stared at him, her eyes as bright as stars, then

she flew at him, beating his chest with her fists as he lifted her off her feet.

'You brute! You never said anything about getting married. I thought you just wanted me to live with you. You never once told me you loved me!'

'But you know I do,' he said with a certainty in his deep voice. 'You've known it all your life. You know I worship you, adore you, and that I've been in love with you for years.'

'Oh, Max! Have you?' she whispered, quite silenced by his words, and he let her slide to her feet, his grey eyes smiling into hers.

'Darling, I've needed you, one way or another, since you were a small, lively nuisance. Now I need you as my wife. Just this once, don't make me a speech. Just say you agree. Will you marry me, Amy, my love?'

'Yes! Oh, yes, Max!' She burst into a storm of tears, and he lifted her into his arms and carried her to the bed, sitting beside her, with his arms holding her tightly to him.

'I just dared not ask you until I had you here,' he confessed softly. 'I had to be quite sure this time. I've learned to tread softly now. So many times I've done the wrong thing, frightened you, annoyed you; this time it had to be right and for ever.'

'Have I done everything wrong, Max, do you think?' Amy asked tearfully.

'Mostly,' he answered, laughing when she glanced up at him with a pained expression on her face. 'Listen,' he said softly, lifting her on to his lap. 'When you were seventeen, I tried to get you to notice me, not just as dear old Max but as *me*! You ran! I had to wait and wait, my heart in my mouth, dreading that you'd find somebody and settle down very nicely. I was devastated to hear about Clive from your aunt Joan on one of her visits, not knowing then, as I do now, that Clive is a self-centred, pompous, righteous . . .'

'You've made your point,' Amy said pertly. 'Please continue.'

'All right,' he laughed. 'I thought that maybe you'd be jealous of Glenys when you came up here. I hoped very much that you would be, anyway. What did you do? You took to her like a sister, helped her, blamed me for every move I made. You actually made me feel like a scoundrel and got me blazing at poor old Seb. For two whole days, I hated the best vet this district has ever had!' He nuzzled against her neck. 'God, you even got me hating the cat because you tried to rescue him. I wanted you so badly I was going out of my mind, and then when I touched you— you ran! Again!'

'I thought . . . I was scared, Max!' she protested. 'When I found out that Glenys and Sebastian were in love and that you'd planned all that, I was so happy. I thought you loved me.'

'I did! I do!' he said violently, giving her a gentle little shake. 'You went straight into my arms that night, sweetheart, and I just lost my head and went too far. I'd only just dragged you back here from London.'

'Where you thought I had a man in the house!' she protested hotly.

'You did!' he said fiercely. 'I was quite prepared to kill him until I came to my senses. Then, on the beach, I really went too far. I thought you'd never recover from it, I was so used to treating you as a child. I wanted to start again, court you, come at things gently, because I knew how you felt by then. You ran again!'

'I saw you, Max,' said Amy, looking down and away from his clear grey eyes. 'I saw you with that beautiful woman. Kitty and I went to the theatre, and I thought you'd come up here. Then you walked in with that woman and I knew you'd lied to me. She was so beautiful I knew you couldn't want me when there was somebody like that.'

Max almost slammed her on her feet and stood, towering over her.

'What woman, for God's sake? I wonder sometimes, my little wretch, if you're quite all there!'

'It's no use pretending, Max,' she said seriously. 'It doesn't matter now. You said you love me and I believe you—but there was a woman.' She described her, and the light dawned in his angry eyes.

'That woman,' he said with a great sigh, 'is the Chairman, if you will, of the theatre committee. She spends the money. I've been asked to do a piece for the foyer. We were there all of ten minutes, and I had to dress up for the occasion because people like that expect to be taken out to dinner. I always add it to the bill, if I don't enjoy it,' he informed her drily. 'I had to get a good look round and then we left. You never said a word about her! Is that why you ran? Is that why you took off to your home stamping ground and nearly killed yourself?'

'It doesn't matter now, Max,' Amy said quickly, a little anxious about the fire that was in his eyes and the stiff annoyance that seemed to be spreading all over him. 'I've said it doesn't matter. There's really no need for us to go over it. I believe you love me.'

'You'd better!' he rasped, grasping her arms and glaring at her. 'If you ever imagine for one minute that I'd ever even look at another woman . . .' He suddenly relaxed all his tense muscles and pulled her into his arms. 'What am I going to do with you, you silly, sweet thing?'

'I'm not at all silly,' protested Amy in a muffled voice, quite relieved to have him back to normal.

'I'll be the judge of that!' Max said firmly. 'I have definite evidence!'

He tilted her face up and kissed her fiercely, holding her head up to his until she could hardly breathe.'

'Let's go!' he said thickly. 'I'm beginning to like it here, and we have to get up to Belmore House and give out the good news. Then you'll want to ring your aunt, and I expect you'll have to ring Bernice and so on.'

'If we didn't go,' Amy said softly, 'we could stay here all night. We could arrive in the morning, all fresh and— and . . .'

'Innocent?' he suggested for her. 'You're just as wicked as I imagined, and while it's an idea that appeals to me very much I don't forget that you recently refused to live here with me, so close to the family. I think, therefore, that I'll keep you at arm's length until we're married.'

He led her downstairs and out of the house, locking the door and then swinging her into his arms and high in the air with a shout of joy, hugging her to him.

'Got you at last, my little bundle of fire!' he exclaimed with a great smile of happiness.

'This isn't arm's length.' Amy pointed out primly, and Max stood her on her feet, taking her hand in his.

'It's near enough, for now.' he said with a grin. 'I imagine that particular decision is one I'm not going to be able to keep, however fast we get married.'

'Why did you take me to Paris?' Amy asked with a

small frown of concentration as they drove to Belmore House.

'To show you I could be close to you without wanting to make love to you,' he said quietly. 'To get to know my grown-up Amy. To set your mind at rest. I damned well managed it, too!' he added proudly.

'I wanted you to make love to me, after I'd got over my fright,' she muttered crossly, and he laughed delightedly.

'I knew that too, darling. It made things quite difficult. I felt really proud of myself later.'

'And how did you feel at the time?' she asked pertly.

'Frustrated!' he confessed. 'As frustrated as I've been for ages, until yesterday,' he added softly, raising her hand to his lips when she blushed wildly.

There was no one at home, and Max seemed to know that perfectly well, because even before they had reached the front steps, he had his key out.

'There's nobody here!' Amy said rather vaguely, looking at him with growing suspicion, and he shrugged, answering her in an equally vague way.

'No, as a matter of fact, Dorothy is in London. She's been spending a few days with your aunt, and Sebastian is away at a conference and—let's see, the housekeeper, it's her day off. That about covers it, if you don't count Smithers, who'll have to be fed.'

'You mean we're alone!' Amy somehow found it alarming, though she couldn't for the life of her think why.

'I have something to show you,' said Max, catching her hand and leading her to the stairs. 'Let's get it over with now, before you have an attack of the vapours.'

He led her to his room and opened a drawer in the bureau.

'I got this in Paris,' he said quietly. 'I've only just worked up the nerve to give it to you. I feared very much that if I'd given it to you before, you'd have run again.'

It was a ring, a sapphire in diamonds, and he slid it on to her finger.

'Sapphire for your eyes,' he said softly, 'diamonds for the sparkle in you that makes you so very special.'

'Oh, Max!' Amy threw her arms around him and hugged him close. 'I'll never take it off!'

He turned her to the figures and photographs that adorned the dark chest by the door.

'Do they still scare you?' he asked quietly. 'I really want them on display in our house, but if they scare you . . .'

'Not now, not when I know how you feel about me,' she confessed. 'You'll be able to do the others now.'

'Yes.' Max wound his arms around her and pulled her back to him. 'The first when you're a bride—my bride—and the next when you're having my child, unless you still find the idea horrific?'

'Oh, no!' Amy sighed. 'I want to be with you just by myself for a while, though, first.

'We're in complete agreement there,' Max murmured against her hair. 'I've waited for a long time. For the moment, I don't feel like sharing you with anyone.' He led her to the door. 'Now, I'm taking you out to dinner, and then I think we'll come back here for the night.'

'I can sleep in my old room,' Amy said dreamily. 'I thought I'd never be able to do that again at one time.'

'I'm not at all sure you will either, my love,' Max murmured, pulling her into his arms. 'After all, I have a room, and then again, there's our own house.'

'But what about the family?' asked Amy, her face flushed as a rose.

'They're quite old enough to take care of themselves,' Max told her with a grin. 'They can find their own beds with no difficulty. In any case,' he added, his lips against hers, 'they'll be so busy racing round to prepare for our very hasty marriage, that nobody will even notice us, providing you just keep quiet and keep out of mischief.'

'And how am I going to do that, being as I am?' Amy wanted to know as he held her tightly.

'I'll think of something!' he assured her as his lips closed over hers.

Coming in June...

Harlequin Presents...

PENNY JORDAN

a reason for being

We invite you to join us in celebrating Harlequin's
40th Anniversary with this very special book we
selected to publish worldwide.

While you read this story, millions of women in 100
countries will be reading it, too.

A Reason for Being by Penny Jordan is being
published in June in the Presents series in 19
languages around the world. Join women around
the world in helping us to celebrate 40 years of
romance.

Penny Jordan's *A Reason for Being* is Presents June
title #1180. Look for it wherever paperbacks are
sold.

PENNY-1

You'll flip . . . your pages won't!
Read paperbacks *hands-free* with

Book Mate • I

The perfect "mate" for all your romance paperbacks

Traveling • Vacationing • At Work • In Bed • Studying • Cooking • Eating

Perfect size for all standard paperbacks, this wonderful invention makes reading a pure pleasure! Ingenious design holds paperback books OPEN and FLAT so even wind can't ruffle pages — leaves your hands free to do other things. Reinforced, wipe-clean vinyl-covered holder flexes to let you turn pages without undoing the strap . . . supports paperbacks so well, they have the strength of hardcovers!

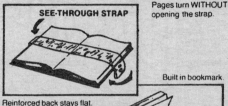

Pages turn WITHOUT opening the strap.

SEE-THROUGH STRAP

Reinforced back stays flat.

Built in bookmark.

BOOK MARK

BACK COVER HOLDING STRIP

10" x 7¼", opened.
Snaps closed for easy carrying, too.

Available now. Send your name, address, and zip code, along with a check or money order for just $5.95 + .75¢ for postage & handling (for a total of $6.70) payable to Reader Service to:

Reader Service
Bookmate Offer
901 Fuhrmann Blvd.
P.O. Box 1396
Buffalo, N.Y. 14269-1396

Offer not available in Canada
*New York and Iowa residents add appropriate sales tax.

BM-G

Harlequin Superromance

**Here are the longer, more involving stories you
have been waiting for... Superromance.**

Modern, believable novels of love, full of the complex
joys and heartaches of real people.

Intriguing conflicts based on today's constantly
changing life-styles.

Four new titles every month.
Available wherever paperbacks are sold.

SUPER-1
